GHOSTS
OF OUR
FATHERS

GHOSTS
OF OUR
FATHERS

MICHAEL RICHAN

DANTULL

By the author

The Bank of the River
A Haunting in Oregon
Ghosts of Our Fathers

GHOSTS OF OUR FATHERS

ISBN-10: 1-49216-038-5 / ISBN-13: 978-1-49216-038-0

Published by Dantull (148113293)

First printing: October 2013

www.michaelrichan.com

For Irene and Rhoda

One

Steven sat bolt upright in bed, frightened.

Someone was in the house.

He grabbed his robe and walked out of the bedroom. He'd done paranoid patrols before, awakened by a sound only to find the house was fine. This time was different. It felt different. He *felt* something was in the house.

The large windows that overlooked Lake Washington were covered with thin blinds that let moonlight into the house, and it was enough to navigate without turning on lights. He walked down the hallway that led from his bedroom towards the living room, wiping the sleep from his eyes and straining them to let in as much light as possible.

Steven rounded the corner of the hallway and slowed, scanning the living room from the hall. There was just enough light to make out all of the furniture as dark shapes. He felt a chill go up the back of his neck; there was a man sitting on one of the chairs.

He froze, unsure of what to do. He couldn't make out any features on the man. He was as dark as the shadows in the room, more of a silhouette. He watched him for several seconds, hoping more of him would be exposed, but he sat still. He was beginning to wonder if it was a mannequin or a statue.

Steven blinked, and the man was standing. He'd gone from a sitting position to a standing position and Steven hadn't seen the movement.

What do I have to defend myself? Steven thought. *I can backtrack to the kitchen and get a knife.*

He walked backwards into the hall, keeping his eyes on the standing silhouette in the living room, watching for more signs of movement. A few steps and he was out of sight of the figure, so he turned and walked back down the hallway. At the end was a turn into the kitchen.

As he entered the kitchen he glanced right to look down into the dining room and living room, to see if the figure was still there. It wasn't.

Shit, he thought. *Where'd he go?*

He looked around the kitchen and his eyes fell on the knife block on the counter. He walked toward it, determined to secure a weapon.

The windows in the kitchen were large and without blinds, as they faced the private backyard. There was a wrap-around deck outside them. More moonlight streamed in here, and Steven could clearly see the knife block and the knife he selected. As he pulled it from the block he glanced up to the window. The man was standing on the deck, just a few feet from him on the other side of the glass.

How did he get out there? Steven thought. *There are two of them!*

Steven backed away from the window, holding the knife. He watched the figure. It didn't move. As in the living room, it looked like a statue. Since it wasn't moving, he stared at it, trying to make out facial features so he could give an accurate description to the police. He couldn't make out any. All of the image was dark. Where the moonlight hit it directly, it was shiny.

He's wearing some kind of body suit, Steven thought.

He blinked, and the figure was gone. He turned to scan the rest of the kitchen, and it wasn't there. He turned to the right to look into the dining room. It was standing three feet from him.

Steven jumped and an involuntary yelp escaped his mouth. He brought the knife up and walked backwards towards the hallway. The figure did not move to pursue him.

Steven's heart was racing a million beats a minute. He could hear his heartbeat in his ears. He felt his mouth suddenly dry, and he licked his lips in response.

I'll back into the bedroom, he thought. *My cell phone is in there, I can call for help.*

When he reached the bedroom door, he opened it from behind and slipped into the room, shutting the door. When he turned around, he saw the figure sitting at the foot of his bed.

He instinctually reached out to turn on the light switch. The room filled with light and the figure vanished. But Steven could still feel it. It was still there, on the bed. He turned the light back off and as his eyes adjusted he saw the dark shape come back into view. It was still sitting at the foot of the bed as still as a statue. It hadn't moved.

It's not a man, Steven thought. *At least, not a normal man.*

Steven was terrified, but this wasn't the first time he'd encountered strange things. Over the course of the past year he'd learned how to deal with ghosts and a variety of manifestations that haunted the house. The first thing to do was to enter the River and see if it would tell him more about who – or what – was sitting on his bed. He kept the knife at arm's length, pointed at the figure.

The River was a moving flow, intangible and invisible to most people, but for those with "the gift" it was something to jump into and exit at will. It offered a different perspective and allowed him to see things that normally weren't visible. He entered the flow, and the light and images in the room changed around him. There was a loud repetitive clicking sound, like the ticking of a clock.

The figure on the bed was now a man, staring at Steven. He looked like he was in his mid-thirties. He had steely blue eyes, a small beard on his chin, and hair that was cut short. He was completely naked. He didn't move. Steven noticed something shiny covering him.

He took a step toward the man. He could see the lips of the man moving, but he couldn't hear him. Steven noticed the man was behind something; something was covering him. Steven realized with horror the man was trapped inside a glass shell shaped like a body.

He walked closer to the figure, and as he did he could begin to hear the man's words. The man couldn't move his body inside the glass shell; it held him rigidly in place at the foot of the bed, but the man's eyes and facial features moved, and his lips. He appeared angry. He was clearly trying to say something to Steven.

Steven put his ear next to the man's lips, listening.

"You're a dead man," the man said from inside the glass shell.

With no observable moment, the man's hand was now around Steven's neck, squeezing. He felt his windpipe being crushed; he couldn't breathe. He reached to the hand to pull it away. It had a smooth surface that wasn't moving, but inside the fingers were shifting, trying to increase the hold. Steven couldn't get a grip on the hand; its surface was too smooth, his fingers would simply slide away from where he was trying to grab. He raised a foot to the glass figure and pushed. He couldn't gain a foothold against the figure either, his foot merely slid off. He felt his head begin to grow light and his vision begin to blur. In desperation he exited the River.

He felt a familiar slicing pain shoot up the back of his skull. The pain often accompanied departures from the River. In this case he had left so abruptly he'd not managed the exit very well, and the pain was particularly sharp. It added to the pain in his throat.

The dark figure was still there, but now he was able to push it away with his foot. It fell back onto the bed, motionless, its arm still raised as though he'd kicked over a mannequin. As Steven held his throat, checking to see if everything felt normal, vertical shafts appeared in the figure exposing the bed covers underneath him. The shafts appeared, disappeared, and shifted, but they kept occurring until the figure was completely gone.

Steven was breathing heavy, wincing from the pain in his head and throat. He stumbled to the bathroom next door and swallowed aspirin. He looked in the mirror to inspect his neck where the figure had grabbed him. It looked OK but it hurt like hell. The clock in the bathroom read 4:30. There was no way he was getting back to sleep considering the adrenaline in his system and the pain he felt.

He walked into the kitchen and sat down on a chair at the kitchen table. In a moment he'd get up and make some coffee, but for now he held his head, waiting for the pain to leave, and thinking through what he just saw.

◊

Steven was too unnerved to go back into his bedroom that morning, but he did manage to fall asleep on the kitchen chair. He awoke around seven, determined to call Roy now that it was a decent hour.

Roy was Steven's father. Roy had the gift too, and he'd been showing Steven how to use his latent skills to deal with some problems that had popped up in his life. Through most of his childhood and into his adult years Steven hadn't been close with Roy, but that all changed when Steven found himself living in a house that was severely haunted; Roy had stepped in and helped Steven resolve the problem. Since then they had become much closer, relying on each other in new ways and building a new relationship.

After the fifth ring Steven remembered that Roy wasn't at home – he'd gone sailing with his friend Dixon and wouldn't be back for a couple of days. Roy didn't have a cell phone and he didn't know if Dixon did either. He felt abandoned. Roy would know what they should do about the figure that threatened him last night, but Roy wasn't going to be able to help for a while.

Eliza, he thought. *I'll call her.*

Steven picked up the phone and called Eliza, remembering her smile from the last time he'd seen her. Eliza lived in Northern California and had helped Steven and Roy deal with a ghost problem in Oregon. She was a strong woman, a little intimidating, but Steven had liked her the moment he met her, and now she was a good friend.

"Eliza?" Steven asked when the phone picked up.

"Yes, this is she," Eliza replied.

"Eliza, it's Steven. How are you?

"Oh, Steven! It's good to hear your voice!" She sounded as if she was groggy.

"Did I wake you?"

"Being honest, yes, you did. But it was time I got up anyway. How are you?"

"Well, that's why I'm calling. I had a rather strange visitation last night."

"A visitation?" Eliza perked up. "That sounds interesting and a little ominous. Tell me about it."

Steven recounted the events of the previous evening, trying to give her as many details as he could remember.

"Steven, I've never heard anything like it," Eliza said. "It's disturbing. I really don't have any idea what to tell you, I'm a little stumped by it."

"Damn, I was hoping you'd have some insight on it, or know what I should do about it. Roy's not around, and I feel a little out of my depth."

"You said you heard a ticking sound once you entered the flow?"

"Yes, it sounded like a loud metronome."

"Well," Eliza said, "I might know someone who could give you more advice. The metronome makes me think of time, and when I think of things time-related, Daniel's the guy. He's a kind of expert on time. He lives in Spokane. I could give you his number?"

"Would you?" Steven asked. "I've got a pen, go ahead."

Eliza relayed the number and Steven jotted it down.

"Do you think it's too early to call him?" Steven asked.

"Let me give him a call first," Eliza replied. "I'll explain some of what you've told me, and tell him you're going to call him yourself within the hour."

"Thank you," Steven said. "When you say he's a time expert, what does that mean exactly?"

"He's like you or me," Eliza said, "he's got the gift, and he practices. But when he was younger he was drawn to aspects of it that related to time, like shifting time, time signatures, time anomalies, that kind of thing. He focused on it over the years, became a sort of expert. It may not help at all, but running it past him won't hurt."

"Great, you're going to call him as soon as we hang up?"

"Yes, I will, and Steven?"

"Yes?"

"Don't worry. We'll get this figured out."

"Thank you, Eliza. Roy is out boating with Dixon and I really didn't know where to turn. I feel better knowing you're in on this."

"I'm with you one hundred percent Steven. I'll do whatever I can."

"Thanks," Steven replied. "I'll call you after I talk with Daniel?"

"Please do."

"Goodbye."

As he hung up Steven realized that having Eliza supporting him lightened him, as though a heavy weight had been removed from his shoulders. Her innate confidence and spirit made him take courage in his situation. He felt lucky to know her.

◊

He waited the full hour before he picked up the phone to call Spokane, hoping that would give Eliza enough time. The voice on the other end of the line was deeply masculine and had a low rumble to it that made Steven want to clear his throat.

"Is this Steven? Eliza said you'd be calling."

"Yes, it's me. Thanks for taking my call."

"Eliza told me a little bit of what's going on, but why don't you start from the top and fill me in. Don't leave anything out."

"Sure," Steven said, and began to recount the events of the previous night once again. He tried to relay every detail he could remember, hoping something would give Daniel a clue that might help.

"Was the glass shell clear or translucent?" Daniel asked.

"It was clear," Steven replied.

"Were there any markings on the glass?"

"I don't recall any. I didn't inspect it all, and I really only saw it for a few seconds."

"Did you notice any smells?"

"Smells?" Steven said. "Yes, there was a smell, it smelled like rope. I've only ever smelled it once or twice before, but I remember the smell from when I was a kid. It smelled like a length of rope my father used to keep in his garage for tying up boats."

"You mentioned vertical shafts," Daniel said. "Can you tell me anything more about them?"

"When a shaft appeared," replied Steven, "you could see the bed behind him. It was like the shaft had removed part of him. Then the shaft would disappear, and a new one would appear, in a different place. Eventually so many appeared his image was gone."

"OK, I have an idea of what it is," Daniel said, "or at least what it partially is. I don't mean to alarm you."

"Trust me, I'm on full alert already. I'd rather hear the full scoop, don't hold anything back."

"All right," Daniel said. "The vertical shafts indicate to me that this being you saw is from some place other than here. Could be the past, could be the future, might be a different dimension, that kind of thing. The shafts are a common visual appearance when the shift is happening."

"And the glass shell?"

"That's a symbolic thing," Daniel said. "He's trapped. His soul is literally trapped. He either bound himself or someone bound him. The glass shell limits the ability of his soul to move or to do things. Some bindings are permanent, others expire after a while."

Steven let the phone hang at his ear, unsure where to go next.

"Listen," Daniel said. "It is dangerous, no question about it. You're being threatened by a soul that's been bound for who knows how long. The fact that the glass is clear tells me the binding is about to end. You need to find out who this is and why he wants to kill you before the binding gives way and he's free. You saw his limits last night, but with the binding gone he will find a way to follow through on his threat, and terrify you in the process."

"Well, that's just great," Steven said. "I feel like I've just been given a terrible prognosis. Why me? I don't even know where to start."

"Listen," Daniel said, "I have a device that might help. If you want, I could come over to your place and try to use it if he appears again tonight."

"Sure, that's kind of you to offer," Steven said. "What does the device do?"

"It's called a collector knife," Daniel said. "If he appears I can use it to collect a piece of him that I can analyze after he's gone. It might tell us who he is and how long the binding will last."

"Perfect," Steven said. "I know Seattle is a long drive, and I appreciate your offer."

"Expect me around 9 p.m.," Daniel said. "And I wouldn't fall asleep before then."

"No, I won't. See you then, and thanks."

Steven hung up and called Eliza to give her the news.

"He knows what he's doing," Eliza said. "You're in good hands, Steven."

"I'm grateful you were able to refer me to him," Steven said. "I'm a little jealous of your network of friends. Claire, Daniel, Joe...I'm sure there's many more."

"They do come in handy," Eliza said. "But you're a friend now too, Steven. I may need you to help me or a friend of mine sometime in the future. We all kind of step in and help each other out when needed."

"Just let me know," Steven said, "and I'm there."

They chatted a bit more about Roy and about Eliza's son Troy, then they hung up. Steven was warmed by his conversation with her and he felt a sense of confidence going into the rest of the day, which passed much more slowly than Steven wanted.

Two

Daniel arrived promptly at 9 p.m., just as he said he would. *Of course,* Steven thought, *he's obsessed with time. Lateness is probably a cardinal sin.*

Steven gave him a quick tour of the house, pointing out the spots where the figure had appeared the night before. Then he showed Daniel the guest bedroom next door to his bedroom. Daniel thanked him, threw his duffel bag on the bed, and began to set up shop.

"Would you like to see the knife?" Daniel asked.

"Sure," Steven said, watching him remove various items from the bag. Daniel pulled out a cloth covered item, stuck his hand under it, then removed the cloth. Daniel's hand was in a grip shape, but what he was holding wasn't visible.

Steven slipped into the flow. The knife became visible immediately. It was about nine inches long, had a curved edge, and tapered from the sharp edge to a thicker top edge that was about a quarter of an inch thick. Daniel demonstrated by waving the knife in the air.

"I'll slice into the shell like this," he said, "and afterwards, remove what it collected here."

The thicker top edge of the knife had a removable cover. Daniel slid the cover back and turned the knife towards Steven. Looking down into the knife from the top Steven could see that it was hollow. "The slice picks up all moments in time – that's what'll give us the history of this thing. It's stored in this chamber until I can sequence them properly and analyze them."

"Wow!" Steven said. "Where did you get this?"

As Daniel continued to unpack, he told Steven about how he'd gathered time-related instruments over the years. Some of them were just collector's items that had some historical value, others were regular tools he used frequently. As he finished they moved into the living room.

"Some of the items I've found," Daniel said, "I've never been able to figure out. I know they're related to time, I can sense it, or I've seen reference to them in a book. But knowing what they do and how to make them work is a lost art in some cases."

"You've got books on this subject?" Steven asked. "Where did they come from?"

"A couple of them came from my uncle. One or two came from friends. They're hard to come by and quite valuable on their own."

"Did your uncle have the gift?" Steven asked.

"Yes, and he kept a book about the things he'd run into, as many of us do."

"My father Roy introduced me to his book several months ago," Steven said. "I was having a problem here in this house with a different set of visitors that were scaring the shit out of me. Roy stepped in to give me a hand and in the process he shared the book with me. Goes back five generations."

"Jesus," Daniel said. "Do you know how rare that is? My uncle's book is just about him, his experiences. I've heard of some that include a grandparent. I've never heard of one that goes back that far within the same family."

"I didn't realize that wasn't normal," Steven said. "I've only recently met others who have the gift, and the subject hadn't come up. I'll have to ask my father if he realizes how important that makes his book."

They talked a while longer about Steven's recent exposure to the River and Roy's tutelage, and about the haunting that Roy had helped Steven eradicate. Then Steven quizzed Daniel more about his past. They talked for an hour, Steven absorbing the new information Daniel offered. Steven had never thought of specializing in a specific area of the gift like Daniel had, and hearing him talk so passionately about his interests fascinated him. He began to wonder how many different aspects of the gift there were to specialize in.

Eventually the discussion drifted back to the matter at hand.

"Did it wake you?" Daniel asked. "When it appeared?"

"I had a sense that something was in the house," Steven said. "That's what got me out of bed."

"What worries me is that it was able to grab you while still in the cage," Daniel said. "If you hadn't been awake first, it might have strangled you in your sleep."

"Well, thanks for that thought," Steven said. "Maybe I shouldn't even go to sleep. If he's going to appear, why does it have to be at 3 a.m.?"

As if on cue, a figure began to materialize next to Steven on the couch. Steven kept on talking, but Daniel interrupted him.

"Steven," he said, "to your right. Look."

Steven turned his head and saw the vertical shafts, slowly thinning. The dark form was back. It was sitting still, looking forward. Steven stood and walked to the other side of the room, away from the figure.

"I'll get the knife," Daniel said, running out of the room.

Steven entered the flow and saw the glass shape with the man inside. He was twisting his head, fighting against the rigid glass form that restricted his movement. His lips were moving, spitting out words that Steven couldn't hear. His eyes were laser focused on Steven, and he could feel the man's anger towards him. There was pure hatred in the man's eyes, and it scared Steven. *If he ever gets out of there*, Steven thought, *he definitely has a bone to pick with me.*

In a blink, the glass form was now standing by the sofa. Steven hadn't seen it rise; it went straight from sitting to standing with no movement in between.

Daniel! Steven thought, *You better hurry!*

He saw the man smile at him from within the glass chamber. Then it disappeared.

He felt the pressure around his neck, like the night before. But this time the hands were coming from behind him. He struggled to turn within the grip, raising his hands to tug at the glass fingers constricting his windpipe. He tried to yell again for Daniel, but nothing would come out.

Steven raised his foot and tried kicking behind. His foot met no resistance as he missed, kicking at air.

Daniel entered the room holding the knife and ran to the glass man behind Steven. He sliced the knife through the figure; it gave no resistance.

It's done! Daniel thought. They both immediately left the flow.

Steven kicked behind him again, and this time he connected with the figure, which released its grip and fell backwards. He turned, gasping for air.

"Are you OK?" Daniel asked, grabbing his arm.

"Yes," Steven said, croaking on the word.

As they both watched, the vertical bars appeared again inside the form, and within a few seconds the image was gone.

"I'll get you some water," Daniel said, releasing his grip on Steven and heading into the kitchen. "I have the sample. The knife worked."

Steven followed Daniel into the kitchen and took the glass Daniel offered. He let the water slowly trickle down his throat, soothing it.

"That was worse than last night," Steven said after he had regained his breathing. "For a moment I thought he had me. I couldn't see him move. He went from sitting still to standing still, and then from standing to behind me, and I couldn't see any movement."

"He's jump cutting," Daniel said.

"Jump cutting?" Steven asked.

"Means he's got a little more control over time than you or I have. Very dangerous, you saw why."

"So now I'm really concerned," Steven said. "What's to stop him from coming back in an hour and surprising me again? Is there anything I can do to protect myself?"

"Yeah," Daniel replied, "there's a couple of things we can try. The main thing is to get this sample analyzed. It'll tell us more about what we're dealing with. Let me see what else we can do."

Daniel walked into the hallway and Steven heard him rustling in the bedroom. Steven walked into the hallway to follow him, but decided instead to visit the bathroom.

He stared into the mirror over the sink, looking at his neck. It seemed normal, but it was extremely painful. He rubbed at it, trying to feel through the surface skin if anything was broken or out of place.

He felt the urge to enter the River, so he slipped into it. He was horrified at what he saw.

Large blue and green patches appeared under his jaw and over his throat. They looked like bruises, but he knew they were more than that. He moved his face closer to the mirror to inspect the discoloration. The surface flesh was moving, shifting places with other flesh around it. At first he thought it was the colors shifting, but as he watched he saw hairs and freckles physically moving. He swallowed and saw his Adam's apple rise and fall, and was disturbed to see the skin over it rearrange itself.

"Daniel?" Steven called.

After a moment Daniel entered the bathroom and looked at Steven examining himself in the mirror.

"Yes? What is it?"

"Enter the River, if you would," Steven said.

Daniel entered the flow and drifted over to Steven.

Jesus Christ! Daniel thought.

Check closer, Steven thought, *in the mirror.* Daniel moved closer to the mirror and examined Steven's skin. He saw it shift and twist, as though something underneath was rearranging the surface.

My god, it's moving, Daniel thought. *What the fuck did he do to you?*

Steven exited the flow and Daniel followed.

"I don't mean to scare you," Daniel said, "but I've never seen anything like that. Did it happen the night before?"

"I don't know, I didn't check."

"I didn't notice anything like it on your neck when you entered the River earlier, when I first showed you the knife," Daniel said. "Your neck looked fine."

"Maybe it heals up," Steven said.

"Maybe," Daniel agreed, though not enthusiastically.

"Any luck with the analysis?" Steven asked, wanting to change the subject to something more optimistic.

"No, in fact I'm afraid I've got some bad news," Daniel said. "Come, let me show you."

Steven followed Daniel into the bedroom next door, where he produced a small box that had a slit about the size of the knife.

"I transferred the sample into this box," Daniel said. "It both holds and analyzes it."

"What's the bad news?" Steven asked.

"When you enter the flow, you can see the symbols here," Daniel said, pointing to the top of the box. "You can then interpret the symbols to discover the make-up of the sample inside. The problem is I'm only getting half the symbols I'd expect. It's confirming that it's a soul cage, and that it's about three days from being completely dissolved, but it's not sequencing the history properly. The symbols that would tell me more, like who it is, why it was bound, they're not showing up. The cage is more complex than this box can decipher. I can't even tell how long it was bound."

"Three days?" Steven said. "And it's dissolving? That means the next time it appears it'll be stronger?"

"I expect so," Daniel said. "But until it's completely free of the cage it doesn't have a lot of energy. It's only able to appear to you now because of the anger of the man inside and the deterioration of the cage. It's better off waiting until the cage is gone, then it'll be free to attack you without restraint."

"Oh great," Steven sighed. "Given how my throat feels now, I'd hate to see what it's like without restraint."

"To get the rest of the information we need on this guy," Daniel said, "I need to take this sample back to Spokane. I have a device there that is more sophisticated. I'm sorry Steven, but it was far too large to bring with me tonight. I'll start back now."

"It's a five hour drive and it's after midnight. You'll go in the morning, after you sleep some. It won't help me to have you wrecked at the side of the road."

"Well, let me at least give you this," Daniel said, handing Steven a small object.

Steven looked at what Daniel had given him. It was a smooth rectangle, about three inches long and half an inch thick. It was pure black and felt like stone. Light didn't reflect off its surface, and it reminded Steven of a miniature version of the monolith from *2001: A Space Odyssey*.

"That'll stop the jump cutting," Daniel said. "Keep it on you all the time from now on and don't let him steal it while you're sleeping. He won't be able to fuck with time if he's within ten feet of it. Let's go back to the mirror, I want to try something."

They both went back to the mirror in the bathroom and entered the flow. Steven noticed the rectangle looked the same in the flow as outside of it.

Place it on the skin of your neck at the bruises, Daniel thought.

Steven did as Daniel instructed. When he removed the object the discoloration was still there but the shifting of the skin had stopped. He repositioned the rectangle over other patches of skin, achieving the same effect. After he had covered all of his neck they both exited the flow.

"Well, that's a relief, thank you," Steven said.

"I'm still not sure what your skin was doing," Daniel said.

"Well, I'll take no shifting over shifting any day. Doesn't seem to help with the bruising though."

"And the bruising is only visible in the River," Daniel noted. "You look fine normally, at least right now."

They walked out of the bathroom and Daniel returned to his bedroom.

"There is one more thing I want you to have," Daniel said. He handed Steven a quart size jar of clear liquid.

"Protection?" Steven asked.

"Yes," Daniel replied, "but not ordinary protection. This is special stuff, designed to resist time-based attacks."

"I've had my father's protection," Steven said, "but it hadn't occurred to me that there might be different…flavors."

"What kind does your dad make?" Daniel asked.

Steven shook his head. "I really don't know. I just assumed that protection was protection, all the same."

"Everyone has their own recipe," Daniel said. "Your dad's is probably his own personal preference. Do you have some around?"

"As a matter of fact, I do," Steven said, walking to the kitchen to find the bottle. He located it hidden behind the cereal boxes in a cabinet.

"Would you mind if I sampled it?" Daniel asked. "In addition to my time studies, I'm a bit of a protection connoisseur."

"Sure," Steven said, handing him the bottle. Daniel raised it to his lips and took a mouthful. After a moment, his eyes went wide, staring at Steven. Then he swallowed it.

"What?" asked Steven. "Too strong?"

Daniel left the room and returned with the collector knife, invisible in his hand. "Could I pour a little into this?" he asked, removing the top and exposing the hollow inside.

"Why?" asked Steven.

"I want to analyze it. I've never tasted anything quite like yours."

"OK," Steven said slowly, wondering what oddity Roy was using. Daniel took the bottle, entered the flow, poured a tiny amount into the top of the blade, then handed the bottle back to Steven. He left the room and returned to his bedroom.

Steven followed him. Daniel raised the knife to the box, but stopped.

"Oh," he said. "I can't analyze this without losing the sample of the glass man. I'll have to wait until I get home and get this sample transferred, then I'll take a look at the makeup of your father's protection."

"So it tastes unusual?" Steven asked.

"Everyone's recipe is a little different, so there's always slightly different tastes. But this one is unique. It doesn't taste like most of them."

"Probably too much vodka," Steven offered.

"It's liberal on the vodka, yes," Daniel said. "But it's not just that. There's something else very interesting going on." He stretched his arms, extending his fingers, feeling the protection moving through his body. "It feels like a general protection, but it feels different. Stronger, more intense and focused. Whoa!" Daniel spread his fingers wide, then curled them into a fist. He smiled.

He turned to look at Steven. "Your dad makes some good shit, my friend!"

Steven smiled. Roy hadn't yet confided his recipe to him, but with Daniel's help he might be able to needle it out of him.

"You realize you won't be going to sleep now for at least another hour," Steven said.

"Don't care," Daniel said. "I have other work I can do. Why don't you try to sleep? I'm going to leave as soon as I wake up in the morning."

"Wake me up before you go," Steven said, "and thanks for your help Daniel. I don't know how I would have figured any of this out without your help."

"Oh, no problem," Daniel said. "And let me tell you, this shot of protection was worth the trip!"

Three

Steven saw Daniel off the next morning and decided to spend some time with Roy's book, which was at Roy's house. As he drove over to Roy's, he imagined his father and Dixon blissfully ignorant of what was happening here at home. *He deserves a break,* he thought. *I can handle this on my own.*

At Roy's he let himself in and put on a pot of coffee. Then he sat at the kitchen table where Roy's book had been sitting for quite a while. Steven began leafing through it.

It was composed of several sections, each one newer and bound to the previous sections. He was the fifth generation of Halls to be reading it, and he expected some day he'd add his own section onto the end. It was already a few inches thick and a little unwieldy to carry, but after hearing Daniel describe how rare such a book was, he resolved that when it passed into his hands he'd make sure it was freshly bound and any delicate pages preserved. Maybe he'd even digitize it as a backup.

As he turned the pages, he kept an eye out for sections that he might understand. Most of the book seemed written in a cryptic way that made no sense. He knew the words were English, but when he read them he couldn't piece together a meaning. Once he had some experience with a subject it gave him a personal context and he found the words began to click in his mind and their meaning cleared. Several sections had opened up to him after he'd been exposed to ghosts and some of the creatures he and Roy had come across recently. He was hoping now that he'd had a brush with the glass man he'd be able to find something in the book that helped him.

He was surprised to find an extended section from Roy's grandfather, Charles. It read clearly to Steven, and he assumed this was because it dealt with something he'd been exposed to. Hoping it was something that might shed some light on his current situation he poured a cup of coffee and read.

January 21 – Teresa has been terrified by Jenny Mae for several nights. I agreed to sit with her and examine the manifestation. She says JM appears every night just as she is trying to fall asleep. I will set up a chair in Teresa's room and observe and see what I can do to help. Teresa looks as though she has not slept in many nights. She tells me she often succumbs to sudden and uncontrollable bouts of vomiting when the child appears. Something must be done. — Just as Teresa said, her head had not been on the pillow for more than a couple of minutes before the ghostly apparition of JM appeared. Since she was only three years old when she passed on, her spirit was about two feet tall, and it materialised, hovering in the air at the foot of Teresa's bed, and it drifted up towards Teresa, who appeared terrified, pulling the bed covers up around her chin in fright. The floating child's face was angry that Teresa wasn't wanting to play, and it repeatedly flew at her with an angry scowl, Teresa cowering her head under the covers each time the child approached. The child worked into a frenzy and eventually let out a wail neighbors in the next county could have heard. Teresa screamed in response. This angered the child more. I rushed to Teresa's side to comfort her and to see if my presence would calm her, since her reactions to the apparition were in my opinion the reason it was accelerating its haunting of her. The ghost child was drifting around the room and when it saw me next to Teresa it became angry again. It began to shake in place, as though it was being rapidly moved back and forth an inch each time, and I felt myself shaking too, in response. I suddenly felt very dizzy and disoriented, and was afraid I might throw up. I slipped into the River and had the impression that I was being physically dislocated. I observed my body and Teresa's body shifting in small, unusual ways, just like the shaking of the ghost child. When I had the good sense to look at my wristwatch, it all came clear to me. The hands of the watch were rapidly moving backwards and forwards. One moment it would read two seconds later, the next several seconds prior. In its anger the ghost child was whipping us backwards and forwards in time, and it was making both Teresa and myself ill, as our mortal minds were not able to handle anything other than the passing of normal sequential time. I could see the child knew this would be the result of its attack upon us. The sicker Teresa became, the more it smiled and giggled. It liked that it could punish her for not playing with her and doing as it wanted. I stood and banished it from the room, but it took several tries before it would leave, and by this time Teresa was violently ill indeed.

January 22 – I gave Teresa a potion just before bedtime that I believe will help alleviate the attacks of the ghost child. Tonight I watched as the child appeared, became angry, and began to shake once again, but Teresa was fine and after a while the child gave up and faded away. I told Teresa we would try again the next day.

January 23 – Again Teresa drank the medicine I provided her and once again as the ghost appeared and tried to whip her back and forth in time it came to naught. Teresa laid back down in bed and attempted to go back to sleep even before JM had disappeared from the room. I believe so long as she takes the precautions I have provided to her, she will be able to get to sleep and stay asleep regardless of what the ghost in her bedroom attempts. She promised me she would continue with the potion, and I agreed to check on her in a week.

January 29 – All is well, JM has given up attempting to haunt Teresa any longer now that Teresa cannot be made ill and the child's vengeance is denied. I will continue supplying Teresa with potion for another month, and after that time, provided JM doesn't appear, she can try forgoing the medicine and see if a new pattern has been developed, hopefully one in which JM doesn't appear at all.

Below this last entry Charles had drawn an image of the ghost child floating at the foot of the bed of a young woman.

Seeing its little feet dangling in the air gave Steven a chill. *I hope I never run into such a thing,* he thought.

The concept of time being used as a weapon was new to him. *Charles must have had a recipe for a time-based protection, like the stuff Daniel gave me,* he thought. He wondered if the recipe was in the book, or if it had been passed down to David and Roy. *Perhaps Roy's protection incorporates it?*

Steven turned the page and kept scanning for more passages that he could interpret. Of all his progenitors, Charles seemed to have the most time-related entries. Just as he found a section on time binding, his phone rang. It was Daniel.

"Steven, I'm sorry to call," Daniel said. He sounded worried.

"Sure, are you in trouble?"

"Kind of," Daniel replied. "I've broken down just outside of Ellensburg. My car isn't the most reliable thing but I thought it would make it. Apparently not. I've got a truck coming but the best they'll do is tow me to Ellensburg."

"I'm on my way," Steven said. "See you in a couple of hours."

Steven left the book and poured the rest of the pot of coffee into a travel mug. Then he locked up Roy's house, got in his car, and headed east on I-90 as fast as he could go.

◊

Steven found Daniel at an auto repair shop in Ellensburg. The car would be finished by the end of the day. They decided to return to Spokane in the meantime so Daniel could finish analyzing the piece of the glass man collected by the knife. Steven would drop Daniel off to pick up his car in Ellensburg on his return drive home.

Steven told Daniel about the passages he'd found in Roy's book as they drove to Spokane.

"I was wondering, since Charles had a protection with some kind of time element in it, perhaps it's been worked into the stuff that Roy uses all the time?" Steven asked.

"Very possibly," Daniel replied. "There's a lot going on in your father's juice, let me tell you. It could very well have some time stuff already in it. I don't know how Roy feels about sharing the family information, but if Charles had a lot of time experiences I would love to read through them. There aren't a lot of works on the subject and I've exhausted all the ones I have; it'd be like fresh blood to me."

"Well, I suppose I could ask him," Steven said. "When he's back."

They talked more about the book and Daniel's take on time bindings before the subject seemed worn out and silence filled the car.

"So," Steven said, struggling to keep the conversation going, "you know Eliza?"

"Yes," Daniel replied.

"How long have you known her?"

"Almost twenty years."

"You'll have to forgive me," Steven said, "the River is all new to me; did you two meet because of that? Do you guys have conventions or something?"

"No," Daniel replied, "we met in a chat room, online. I think our mutual interests sparked things, but there was an attraction there for sure."

"Oh, you two were a thing?" Steven asked.

"For a while," Daniel said. "Troy's my son."

Whoa, Steven thought.

"Eliza didn't tell you?" Daniel asked. "From the look on your face, I'm guessing she didn't."

"No, she didn't," Steven answered. *So what?* Steven thought. *It doesn't matter. Don't overreact.*

"You know how you can really like someone," Daniel said, "but could never live with them? That's me and Eliza."

"So you really like her?"

"Who doesn't?" Daniel said. "She's immediately likeable. Everybody loves her. I just couldn't live with her. And we haven't had a 'thing' for many years now. We're friends. More like professional acquaintances than anything. She has a lot of those."

"And Troy?" Steven asked.

"I don't understand that part," Daniel said. "I offered child support, I offered to stick around and be his dad, but she didn't want any of that. She wanted to raise him entirely on her own without my involvement. I wasn't too happy with that arrangement at first, but she insisted. I decided to honor her requests and stay out of his life. I've only met him once. That was a hard day, let me tell you."

"I'll bet," Steven said. He thought about his son, Jason, and couldn't imagine not being involved with him. But then, Jason was at college and was busy with school and friends. He didn't see him very often, which seemed like the right thing to do, to let him live his own life without a lot of interference. Hell, he'd been pretty distant from Roy up until this year, when Roy stepped in to help him. In reality he hadn't been all that close with his own father in the past, or even with his son now. *Best not to judge,* he thought.

Once they reached Daniel's house in Spokane, Daniel set about analyzing the sample he had stored in the box. He placed it in a much larger wooden box, about the size of an old 27" television. After several minutes he began to see the symbols he was looking for.

"Far more complex," Daniel said, interpreting the symbols. "But we're getting there. Can you write this down, Steven, while I dictate? It will be easier."

"Sure," Steven said, sitting at a small desk and arranging some paper for him to record Daniel's comments.

"His name is...Frank Wilmon..." Daniel said, spelling the last name. "He's been trapped since...1933."

"Eighty years!" Steven said under his breath.

"He died in 1974," Daniel continued. "The cage was constructed by..."

Daniel paused.

"…Sean and Garth Wilmon, his sons, ages seven and five at the time." Daniel turned to look at Steven. They both seemed surprised.

"That wasn't what I was expecting," Daniel said.

"Me either," Steven replied. "Is there more?"

"Yes," Daniel said, returning to the symbols. "Sean passed away. But Garth is still alive."

"Does it say where he is?" Steven asked.

"No," Daniel replied, "but you can usually find that out in other ways, like the internet."

"Can I use this computer, here?" Steven asked, referring to the computer sitting next to him on the desk.

"Sure," Daniel said. He returned to the symbols, looking for more information.

Steven began searching for Garth Wilmon. It didn't take long to locate a phone number which had a 360 area code.

"Found it," Steven said, "looks like the Olympia area. I'm going to give it a call."

Daniel didn't respond, immersed in reading more symbols.

Steven dialed the number. "This is Tall Pines, how may I direct your call?" came the voice that answered.

Steven paused. Tall Pines? Was it a hotel? "Can you connect me to Garth Wilmon?" he asked.

"I'm sorry, Mr. Wilmon isn't in his room right now. Would you like to leave a message?"

"Sure, but before I do, can you tell me what Tall Pines is? Are you a hotel?"

"We're an assisted living care facility, sir," came the voice on the phone.

Ah, of course, Steven thought. "What are your visiting hours?"

"Anytime between 7 a.m. and 10 p.m., every day."

"Yes, would you leave Mr. Wilmon a message?" Steven asked. "Tell him that Mr. Hall needs to meet with him, and I'll be there tomorrow morning first thing."

"Can I tell him what it's regarding?"

Steven thought. "Yes, tell him it's regarding Frank."

"OK, I'll leave this message for him."

"Thank you," Steven said, hanging up.

Steven turned to Daniel, who was focused on the readout once again. "There's no way I'll make it to Olympia before 10 p.m. tonight when they stop visiting hours," he told him.

Daniel looked up. "Your dad's protection is off the charts. It has more variants than any I've ever seen, and at the same time it's the most pure I've ever seen. Impressive."

"Variants?" Steven asked.

"Different elements of the recipe that protect against specific things. The most common protection is a generic protect-all kind of mixture. People who know what they're doing can add variants that make the protection strong in specific areas, like the one I gave you; it has time protection variants. Your dad's protection — it has dozens of variants, some I've never seen before."

Steven didn't know exactly what to make of this information, but he felt a little pride well up in him. Roy had always been just a father, and a distant one at that. Learning that Roy had the gift had distinguished him in Steven's eyes and over the course of the past year Steven had learned that his father knew far more than he could ever imagine. But to hear that he was distinguished even within these esoteric circles surprised him.

"You've had it, I presume?" Daniel asked.

"Several times," Steven answered. "When he and I were working on a few problems."

"If he ever decides to market that stuff," Daniel said, "he'll make a fortune. I could spend the next ten years trying to duplicate it and wouldn't get close."

"I'll tell him that," Steven said, wondering which day Roy had said he planned on returning from his boat trip with Dixon.

Daniel's phone rang and he stepped into another room to answer it. Steven took the opportunity to look around Daniel's workshop a little more. It reminded him of Eliza's but without the feminine touches. There was no comfortable sitting area, just tables loaded with projects and devices. Along one wall there were bookcases with objects placed on them about a foot apart from each other. They seemed to be on display rather than for use.

Daniel returned from the other room. "That was the auto place in Ellensburg. The car's done. Oh, I see you've found the unknowns."

"I thought you might call them the antiques, but based on the condition of some of them I was wondering if they were just art," Steven said.

"The term 'antique' doesn't mean much in my world," Daniel said. "Those are the devices that I haven't figured out yet. Some of them I've had for years. I may never figure them out. But every now and again I come across something that unlocks what one of them does, and then I'm glad I kept it."

Steven surveyed the contraptions. They seemed like odd pieces of junk, without any value or technological elements. One even looked like an old rusty can.

"Jump in," Daniel said. "You'll see what I mean."

Steven entered the flow and the objects transformed. The rusty can looked like a round ball with deep etchings. Several of the objects had a light yellow hue to them. The hue pulsed on a few of them. He slipped back out of the River, feeling the slight stab of pain in the back of his neck.

"Wow," Steven said, turning to Daniel. "You've just collected them over the years?"

"Some I came across, a couple I bought and some were gifts," he said. "When people know you collect a certain thing, they feel compelled to give you more of that thing for your birthday or Christmas. I've got boxes of the duplicative crap I've been given by well-meaning friends. My work and collection is more specialized now, and most of these objects on the shelves are rare."

"If I ever decide to give you a gift," Steven said, "it will be a CD or something. No time objects."

"Thank you," Daniel said. "Unless, of course, you want to give me some really cool and rare time object. Please don't hesitate in that case."

"How would I know if it was cool or rare?" Steven asked. "I'm guessing you can't determine the value of these items on the internet?"

"Ah, giving gifts to collectors is a bitch, isn't it? A CD will be fine."

Four

Steven drove back to Seattle, dropping Daniel in Ellensburg to retrieve his car. On the way, Steven quizzed Daniel more about the time objects and their capabilities. Daniel had some interesting stories to tell and the two hour drive went quickly.

As they pulled into Ellensburg, Daniel turned to Steven.

"Do you mind if I tag along?" he asked. "On your visit to Olympia?"

"No, I wouldn't mind at all," Steven replied. "You've been extremely helpful so far. It would be nice to have you along."

"I have to admit I'm intrigued," Daniel said. "I'd like to hear what he has to say."

"Sure, you can stay at my place tonight," Steven said, "and we'll drive to Olympia first thing in the morning. Should we just continue on and I'll bring you back out to get your car?"

"Oh no," Daniel said, "that's way out of your way. I'll pick my car up now and follow you. That way you won't have to drive back out here."

Steven drove Daniel to the auto repair shop and dropped him off. Soon they were back on the interstate, convoying to Seattle.

As he drove, observing Daniel's car in the rear view mirror, Steven was grateful Daniel was available and willing to help. He felt a little lost without Roy around. He'd come to rely on his father far more than he realized. *What a change,* he thought. *I hardly ever see him for most of my life, now I miss the bugger when he's gone for a week.*

He tried to remember what day Roy said he'd be back. *He said he'd be gone a week,* Steven thought. *It's been about that. Maybe he's back today?*

Certainly Roy would have a perspective on this. Roy always had a perspective. He could be cranky and crass, but his heart was in the right place and he'd been there to help Steven when he needed him most. Steven had come to rely on him.

What happens when he passes on? Steven thought, then immediately felt guilty for considering the idea. *I shouldn't be thinking about that. Drop the subject.*

They arrived in Seattle around midnight.

"Let's turn in," Steven said, "I want to be on the road to Olympia by 6 tomorrow."

"Sleep with that object close," Daniel said. "Don't leave it on your nightstand where our visitor might be able to take it from you."

"I think I have a solution," Steven said. He went to the bathroom and removed some ankle tape, then he bound the rectangle Daniel had given him around his arm. The elastic of the tape kept it firmly in place. He showed Daniel his arm.

"Perfect," Daniel said. "And you have the protection I gave you?"

"Yes," Steven said, "I'll down it just before I get into bed."

"All right. Wake me up if he shows up."

"Will do. Goodnight."

Steven tried to sleep, but he was still a little wired from the drive and the protection surging through his body didn't make it any easier. He wished he had Roy's book so he could read more until he felt sleepy. It didn't feel right to remove the book from Roy's house without his permission.

He slipped into bed and turned off the light. He felt around his neck. He could still feel the pain from his encounter with the glass man the night before. He hoped Daniel's object would help if the man appeared tonight. Anticipation of the meeting was another thing keeping him awake. He tried several sleep techniques he'd learned over the years but none of them were working.

He turned over in bed, looking up at the ceiling. Faint moonlight coming in through his bedroom window lit the wall to his right. The shadow of the glass man was upon it; he turned to his left and the figure was at his bedside. Steven instinctively raised his arm, bandaged with the object inside, to his neck.

The glass man stood as a statue, like before. Steven slipped into the flow.

"It's almost time," the man said.

Steven was surprised to hear the voice. *The glass must be thinning,* he thought. *Time for what?*

"Time to pay you back," the man said.

I haven't done anything to you, Steven thought.

"I paid with eighty years," the man said. "You're going to pay with your life."

The glass moved, but this time Steven could observe the movement. The glass man moved his hand inches from Steven's face, then stopped. The man's brow furrowed, frustrated. "What?" he said, confused.

Steven didn't respond. The man didn't seem to clue in that Steven had taken defensive steps.

The man growled. The glass moved again, this time to a different pose. Same result, the man's hand stopped inches from Steven.

The man moved around the bed to Steven's other side. He observed Steven's head following his movement, and realized his ability to surprise Steven was gone. He let out another frustrated growl. Then the vertical panes appeared, and within a few seconds he had left the room.

It worked, Steven thought, exiting the flow. If he follows the same pattern he won't be back again tonight.

He considered waking Daniel but then decided against it. The visit was over; he could tell him about it in the morning. Time now to sleep. Six a.m. was only a few hours away.

Steven instead tossed and turned, adrenaline now mixing with the protection. It was going to be a tough night.

◊

On the drive to Olympia, Steven related the incident to Daniel.

"Why didn't you wake me up?" Daniel asked.

"He had come and gone within thirty seconds," Steven said. "And the good news is, your protection worked. He tried several times to come at me and was stopped. He was clearly frustrated by that. He eventually gave up and blipped out."

"Well, I'm glad of that," Daniel said.

"He did say 'I paid with eighty years, and you're going to pay with your life.' I wasn't sure what to make of that."

"Well," Daniel offered, "the eighty years must mean the time binding. If the binding was to make him pay for something, like a punishment, I wonder what he did."

"That'll be agenda item number one with Garth," Steven said.

Traffic was still light so early in the morning, and they soon found themselves navigating to the Tall Pines facility in Olympia, a few minutes after 7 a.m.

They walked into the lobby. It was large, open, and beautifully furnished. There were several couches in different areas of the room, and several seniors were moving through to a larger room in the back where breakfast was being served.

Wow, this is much nicer than I imagined, Steven thought.

He noticed a woman sitting behind a beautifully carved desk. She was younger and had a name badge. Steven assumed she was the receptionist. As he approached the desk, her desktop sign read "Concierge."

"Excuse me," Steven said to her, smiling. "We're here to meet with one of the residents. Are you the person we should talk to?"

"Yes, I can help you," she said, smiling back. "Who were you meeting?"

"Garth Wilmon," Steven answered.

"That's Mr. Wilmon over there," she nodded, referring to a man sitting in a winged back leather chair on the other side of the room. "He's expecting you."

"Thank you," Steven said, turning to walk to towards the man in the chair.

As they approached, Garth Wilmon stood. "You must be Steven," he said.

"I am," Steven said, "Steven Hall. And this is Daniel..." Steven realized he'd never learned Daniel's last name.

"Simmons," Daniel offered, sticking his hand out towards Garth, who held it and gave it a shake. "Daniel Simmons."

"Nice to meet you both," Garth said. "Would either of you like breakfast?"

Steven and Daniel turned to each other. They had left the house so quickly they had only brought coffee. Steven's stomach was beginning to growl.

"Are you going to have breakfast?" Steven asked Garth.

"Well," Garth replied, "I am, and I've made arrangements for it to be served to us over there." He pointed to a small alcove. An elderly couple passed behind Steven and Daniel on their way to the dining room and Garth gave them a wave.

"Sure," Steven said. "That would be nice."

This was not what I was expecting from an assisted care facility, Steven thought.

They all walked over to the alcove. It was lined with bookcases and had a fireplace with a small fire rolling inside. There was another leather chair and a small sofa. Garth took the chair. On the small coffee table between them was a large art book from the Carnegie museum in Pittsburgh. As soon as they sat, a waiter appeared and poured coffee for each of them and took their breakfast order.

"They'll make you pretty much anything," Garth said. "No menu. All the normal stuff."

They each gave the waiter an order and he departed. Although Steven could see people passing by on their way to breakfast, the alcove was relatively private.

"Your message was intriguing and not very informative," Garth said.

"Sorry about that," Steven said. "I needed to get your attention, because I need your help."

"And how can I help you?" Garth asked, pouring cream into his coffee.

Months ago Steven might have danced around the subject. Now he felt the direct approach was the best. "Over the past few days," Steven said, "I've been harassed by your father, Frank."

"Stepfather," Garth said, taking a sip of coffee. "And that's quite impossible, since he's been dead for forty years."

"It's not his physical self threatening me," said Steven. "It's his soul."

Garth sat his cup down and looked at Steven defensively. "Is this a shakedown? Despite all this," he said, waving his hand, "I don't have money. It's all locked away in my children's hands, so you're wasting your time."

"No, nothing like that," Steven said. "I'm only after information. Your stepfather has threatened to kill me. I'm trying to figure out why."

"You're speaking about him in the present tense," Garth said. "You realize you sound like a lunatic?"

"I'm betting you know I'm not," Steven said.

Garth eyed Steven again, giving him the once over.

"Frank's soul has been caged for the past eighty years," Daniel said. "Even though he passed away forty years ago, his soul is still very much alive. The problem is the cage is now deteriorating, and he'll be on the loose within a few days. And he appears to be pissed off."

The color drained from Garth's face. He looked from left to right and back again, seeming to be searching for a way out of something. "I didn't think there was a time limit," he muttered.

"What?" Steven asked. "Did you say a time limit?"

Garth looked up. "Yes, I didn't think there was a time limit."

"On Frank?" Steven asked.

"Yes, on Frank," Garth said.

"So you know what I'm talking about?" Steven said.

Garth sighed. "Yes," he said. "I think I do."

The waiter appeared with their food. Garth paused while the plates were passed around and more coffee was poured. Once the waiter left, Garth took a bite of a bagel. He chewed it slowly and deliberately, as though he was using the time to pull up memories of Frank.

"It's a rather long story, Mr. Hall," Garth said.

"Please, call me Steven," he replied.

"All right, Steven then. It's a long story, and it happened a long time ago. If you hadn't noticed, I'm rather old now, and my memory isn't what it used to be. But I'll go back if you want me to."

"It's more of a case of needing you to," Steven said. "I believe when the cage is gone, he will try to kill me. He's already tried and failed."

"All right then," Garth said. "I believe you. My stepfather was an evil man. Let me tell you what happened back in 1933."

Five

Sean had been hungry all day from the moment he'd woken up. He'd eaten a couple of spring onions while working in the fields with his stepfather, but they were still young and bitter and not very satisfying. Still, it felt good to have something in his mouth to chew. Since his mother died, that feeling had become increasingly rare.

The years with his mother now seemed like a distant dream, a paradise. Then, he and Garth played at home all day while she worked around the house. They had a large house and a large lawn, and he and Garth would be sent outside by their mother when she couldn't stand them in the house anymore. In the yard they would drag an old red wagon around and try to play badminton with an old set of rackets that were missing most of the strings.

Sometimes they would venture into the old stand-alone garage in the far corner of the backyard, but only to grab a rake or ball or the badminton set. They were both afraid of the garage. The open door entrance allowed the afternoon light to shine into part of it, and they limited themselves to the areas where the light fell. They had ventured deeper into the garage once, towards the back of it where the heavy doors had once swung open to allow a car to drive inside. There were dirty windows in those doors, and they didn't let in much light. The doors hadn't been opened in a long time, and the garage was now full of cast-off junk from the house, their mother and stepfather preferring to park the family truck on the street. The one time they tried exploring back there they had both become frightened. It was now an unspoken agreement to limit their garage boundaries to the area immediately inside the door with the light.

There were other areas in the house that were frightening, too. They slept together in a basement bedroom, and the basement itself was dark and unsettling. Every night when forced to bed, they'd descend the wooden steps from the kitchen, and make a quick sharp turn into their bedroom at the base of the stairs, shutting the door quickly behind them. The rest of the basement was largely unexplored, a collection of unfinished sections. In a far corner was a large pile of coal, used to feed a furnace. They never played downstairs outside of their bedroom.

Inside the bedroom things were less scary, but being a basement bedroom with a tiny window near the ceiling it didn't have a lot of light. There was a dim overhead fixture which helped some, but not much. Even in the middle of the day with the light turned on it felt dark.

They shared a double bed pushed into a corner of the room. Laying in the bed at night, Sean and Garth would point out the things in the room that calmed them, like the baseball pennants they'd arranged on the walls and a bobblehead doll that sat on a dresser. They were both afraid of a hole in the ceiling by the open closet, which was tucked into the space under the wooden stairs that led down from the kitchen. The hole was about a foot across. Neither boy knew how the hole got there. They avoided looking at it, especially at night, because whatever might emerge from it was too horrible to consider.

Their mother would listen to their fears and try to console them. She was who they ran to when anything needed solving. But after their mother died, things changed. Their stepfather Frank became unfriendly to everyone, especially Sean and Garth. With their mother not there to stop him, he would drink and become mean. After a while Frank stopped any pretense of being a loving father and settled into a daily pattern of work followed by a few hours of liquor-induced stupor. Sean and Garth had learned to make themselves scarce during the hours between, when he was at his meanest.

Several months ago Frank had begun taking Sean and his brother into the onion fields to work every day. The boys were expected to help irrigate and weed the rows. It was tough work for young children. Sean had learned early on that playing with Garth while they worked was not a good idea. The sun beat down on them relentlessly, and having a drink of water every now and again was essential to staying conscious. When Frank found them playing instead of working, he'd punish them by eliminating their breaks, which meant they couldn't stop for water. It only took once or twice having to go thirsty for hours while on his knees pulling weeds for Sean to know it was better to leave Garth alone and stick to the chores.

This evening Frank had been swearing and yelling ever since he raised the bottle to his lips. He and Garth had decided to play outside so Frank wouldn't notice them. They instinctually played quietly, knowing that drawing attention from Frank while he was drunk was a bad idea. Neither he nor Garth had any food throughout the day, and Sean was hoping he could sneak inside the kitchen and grab something while Frank wasn't paying attention, so he and Garth could eat.

He tried to convince Garth to wait in the backyard for him to return with something, but Garth said he was starving and would go with him to help carry out more food. Sean didn't think having his five-year-old brother in tow would help make his task any easier, but Garth was insistent.

They crept up the cement steps that led to the kitchen door. They both knew how to get the kitchen door open without a sound. Sean could hear Frank swearing and cussing elsewhere in the house; it sounded like he was lying in his bedroom, which was a comfortable distance from the kitchen.

Sean lead the way, with Garth quietly tip-toeing behind him. Sean knew the best food would be in the icebox. He was after the bread, and Frank always kept it there. After carefully avoiding the floorboards that he knew would creak, he tried to open the icebox latch slowly so it wouldn't make its normal clicking sound.

Once he had the door open, inside they both saw a heel of bread, about two inches thick. Sean turned to look at Garth, who smiled back and nodded. This would be their prize if they could successfully sneak it out of the house without Frank hearing them.

Sean grabbed the chunk of bread and handed it to Garth, then he shut the icebox door, going as slowly as he could to avoid any noise. When he was done, they both turned to tip-toe back to the kitchen door.

"So you're goddamn thieves now?" Frank said from the doorway that led to the living room. "Sneaking in here like common thieves?"

"We haven't had anything to eat today," Sean said, pleading. He could see the bottle in Frank's hand; it still had a couple of inches of brown colored liquid inside, but enough was gone for Sean to know he was arguing with the devil.

"Oh, that's right – you gotta eat, I know that," Frank said. He sat down in a kitchen chair next to the kitchen table, positioning the chair to face the boys.

"Let's see who wants it the most," Frank said. "Do you want it more than your brother?"

Sean stared at Frank, unsure of what he was asking. Garth held the bread to his chest a little more tightly. He wanted to take a bite of it, but was afraid to do it in front of Frank.

"Looks like your brother stole all the dinner," Frank said to him.

"He'll share some with me," Sean said.

"No, he won't," Frank said. He waved his hand at Garth. "Give me that, boy!"

Garth knew better than to go against Frank. He walked over to where Frank sat and placed the bread in Frank's hands. As he turned to walk back to Sean, Frank raised a foot and kicked Garth squarely in the back. Sean saw Garth's frame bend into an arc as the foot made contact with him, the surprise and hurt spread across his face, and then his body was propelled forward towards Sean. He caught him just before he made contact with the kitchen cupboards. Garth began crying.

"This bread," Frank said, "is only enough for one thief. Only one of you can have it. No sharing."

Sean felt the pit in his stomach widen.

"Who wants it?" Frank asked.

Sean and Garth looked at each other. They both weakly said "I do" at the same time.

"The winner gets it," Frank said to them. "Fight him for it." He took another long throat full of the booze. Both boys stood in the kitchen, still. They weren't sure they understood him.

Frank looked at Garth. "Fight him for it! You can't both have it. Hit him. Give him a good punch. Beat him up, and it's yours." Frank pulled a piece of the bread off and ate it. "Sure is good. I'm gonna wind up eating it all if you don't fight him for it, then you'll get none."

Sean looked at Garth; he could see the hunger in Garth's eyes. He wanted Garth to have the bread, but he knew Garth would never start the fight. So he pushed him hard enough that he fell to the floor.

Predictably, this enraged Garth. He leapt to his feet and charged Sean. Sean pretended to fight back, but at seven years old he could easily have beaten Garth had he wanted to. Garth threw punches and Sean took them. He let Garth climb on top of him, swinging. Garth was crying, partly from pain, partly from hunger, and partly from anger. Sean felt his little fists pounding into his stomach. He raised his hands to defend himself but let Garth make contact with each punch. Sean felt like doubling over, but he couldn't with Garth on top of him. He tried to grab Garth's arms to stop the swinging, but Garth had turned into a machine, running on automatic, starving and determined to have the bread. Sean felt the pain from the punches combine with his own hunger and humiliation at having to let his brother do this to him just to satisfy Frank. As

Garth's punches slowed, he started to cry and rolled away from Frank so he couldn't see him, pushing Garth off.

"Pathetic," Frank said. "What a pussy."

Frank tossed the bread onto the floor where Garth lay, panting and sobbing. "Here you go. Eat it now, in front of me. I wanna make sure he doesn't get any."

Garth grabbed the bread and began chewing it. Sean quieted his crying; he didn't want either of them to hear how angry and upset he was. After a few moments, he could hear Frank stand up.

"Now, get out of here!" Frank yelled, walking towards them. Garth was on his feet and out the kitchen door immediately. Sean raised himself up on one arm but felt the pain in the side of his abdomen where Garth had made several successful punches, and he winced. Frank walked over to him and kicked his arm out from under him; he went back down. He grabbed his arm, afraid it might be broken.

"Out," Frank said. "Or the next one'll be on your ass."

Sean raised himself up despite the pain and ran towards the door. As he walked down the steps that led into the yard, he saw Garth disappear into the open door of the garage.

He stumbled through the backyard, walking towards the garage. He knew he needed to talk to Garth. He wanted more than anything to fall down on the cool grass and just rest, but he could hear Garth sobbing in the garage and wanted to go to him, and he felt like putting distance between himself and Frank.

As he walked through the door opening, the smell of old wood that had been baking in the sun greeted him. The garage had always smelled like this, old and musty and dry. Even though the sun was starting to set and it was getting a little darker outside, the garage still retained the heat from the day.

Garth was at the back of the lit area, under a wooden bench. "I'm sorry," he said as he gulped air between sobs.

"It's OK," Sean said, sitting down on the floor, holding his side.

"Did I hurt you?" Garth asked.

"No," Sean lied, "a little runt like you couldn't hurt a fly."

Garth didn't reply and kept crying. Sean leaned back, thinking it might help the pain. It didn't.

"What are you going to eat?" Garth said, still under the bench.

"I guess nothing," Sean said.

"We could sneak in later," Garth offered. "We could sneak up in the middle of the night, after he's gone to sleep."

"Maybe we'll do that," Sean said, rolling over onto his side. He looked into the back of the garage, into the area where they never went. His eyes rested on the piles of junk. There was just enough light still coming through the door that he could see the various pieces of it.

"I'll do it," Garth said. "I won't get caught. He can't hear me."

Sean thought he'd reply to Garth, telling him that was a bad idea, but instead he blinked his eyes, unsure if he was seeing what he thought he was seeing. Sticking out of the pile of junk was a hand. It was outstretched towards him, as though it was holding something. It looked pale white and he couldn't see anybody attached to it. He thought it might be part of a dead body. He felt the hair on his neck rise.

"Shh," he said to Garth. "Be quiet for a second."

Garth quieted his crying and Sean pushed himself back up into a seated position. The new viewing angle confirmed it was indeed a hand. Its palm was open as though it was offering him something, but he couldn't see what it was.

"Garth, come over here," Sean said. "Be quiet."

Garth crawled along the garage floor to where Sean sat. When he reached him, he sat next to him, mimicking Sean's pose.

"Do you see it?" Sean asked.

"What?" Garth asked.

"Look!" Sean said, nodding towards the back of the garage. Garth raised his head and wiped his eyes.

"Yeah," Garth said. "What is it?"

"It's a hand," Sean said.

"Whose hand?" Garth asked.

"Let's find out," Sean said, crawling forward towards the back of the garage. The hand remained motionless, extended and cupped as though it was holding something. Sean couldn't see anything it was holding, but Garth reached forward to touch it.

"There's something in its hand," Garth said. "I could feel it."

"I don't see anything," Sean said.

"Try yourself," Garth said.

Sean reached forward. As he pressed a finger into the space above the hand's palm, he felt resistance against something soft.

Garth grabbed Sean's arm. "Look, Sean!" he said, pointing to a space in the junk pile. A small white face stared out at them. It looked like a baby's face, but after a moment it looked more like a child their age.

"Try it," the face said.

Sean looked at Garth. His cheeks had been red from crying, but now the color drained from his face. They both tensed, feeling the need to bolt from the garage.

"It's food," the face said.

Sean stared back at the face, which seemed to look older now. He looked back at the hand. "I don't see anything," Sean said.

"Take it anyway," the face said. "You're hungry."

As though the words themselves caused his stomach to growl, Sean felt the stab of hunger hit his stomach and he knew he'd eat anything to make the pain go away. He reached towards the hand and wrapped his fingers around whatever it was holding. As he pulled his hand back, his fingers were spread apart as though he was holding a baseball.

"Wow," Garth said. "It's invisible!"

"Eat it," the face said again.

"What is it?" Sean asked, looking back at the face. Now it looked like the face of a toddler.

"Does it matter?" the face replied.

Sean thought about this and decided it didn't. He moved the invisible thing to his mouth. Once he felt it press against his lips, he opened his mouth and took a bite. He felt it enter his mouth, and he chewed it. It didn't taste like anything, but once it was in his mouth and he could feel it inside, he relaxed and felt better. He swallowed and felt it go down his throat. As it hit his stomach, he felt a warmth radiate out from his chest. He felt the pain in his stomach subside and the pain in his ribs lighten.

"Go on," the face said.

He took another bite, and then another. Garth watched him. It looked to Garth as though he was fake eating. "Can I have a bite?" Garth asked. He felt guilty for asking having already downed the bread, but he was fascinated by what he saw Sean doing, and wanted to know if it was real.

"Sure," Sean said, handing him what was left after several bites. Garth extended his hand and Sean moved his palm next to Garth's, turning over his hand and dumping what remained into Garth's palm. Sean felt full.

Garth took a bite and after swallowing, smiled. He immediately felt better.

"He is a bad man," the face in the junk pile said to them.

"He is mean," Garth replied.

"Who are you?" Sean asked. "I'm Sean, and he's Garth."

"I'm just a baby," the face said. As they watched, the face's mouth slowly opened and its eyes widened. It sputtered and gasped, trying to breathe, shuddering. Its lips turned blue and its eyes began to bulge and roll upward, leaving only white. Garth grabbed Sean's arm, afraid of what he was seeing. Then the shuddering stopped and it was still. The eyes rolled back down, and it stared past them, no longer seeing. It faded, leaving only a dark hole in the junk pile.

"Hello?" Sean said.

Garth stood and approached the pile. He walked around the edge of it, studying it, trying to see the face. "He must be inside there," Garth said, looking for entrances or gaps that might allow someone to crawl in or out.

"Here!" Garth said from the back of the pile. "Here's a hole!"

Sean rose off his knees. He no longer felt any pain in his side; the substance he'd eaten had not only resolved his hunger but taken away the pain of his fight with Garth. He walked around behind the junk pile where Garth was standing. They were now in the back corner of the garage, a place they never ventured. The light was very dim, and it was hard to make anything out.

"Look," Garth said, dropping to his knees. "He's in here!" Garth disappeared inside a small hole next to the wall of the garage, barely big enough to accommodate him.

"Wait!" Sean said, but Garth was already gone.

A moment later, from inside the junk pile, Garth screamed.

Sean panicked. He was afraid for Garth, but Garth screamed all the time. He was more afraid Frank might hear the scream, come find them, and beat them. Sean dropped to his knees and looked into the hole Garth had crawled into. He was met with Garth's posterior rapidly approaching his face.

Sean pulled back and Garth's feet and legs emerged from the hole. He was rapidly backing out of it. As his body cleared the hole he leapt to his feet and ran to hug Sean. They both looked at the hole he had emerged from.

"Run!" Garth said, pushing him.

Sean didn't run. He strained his eyes to see the hole, to see what would come out of it. He was expecting a rat. He'd dealt with them before. If it was, he'd stomp on it. A couple of good kicks was all it took to stop a rat.

What emerged from the hole wasn't a rat. It was large, and it looked more like the head of a goat. It had two long horns. It had a long, flexible neck, like a snake, but thick. Once the head had emerged from the hole, it turned to look at Garth, who grabbed his brother tightly. Its eyes were dark red and the glow from them lit the garage with a hue that made the walls look like they were on fire.

Sean knew he should follow Garth's advice and run, but the creature that emerged from their junk pile was so fantastic that he was mesmerized and felt compelled to examine it. The neck continued to extend out of the hole and the goat head began to rise until it was as tall as Sean. The head moved toward them and Sean took a step back, dragging Garth with him. The mouth of the goat began to open. Inside was fire, a swirling mass of red, orange and yellow. Smoke came out of the goat's nostrils. The fire extended out of the mouth and towards Sean and Garth.

Garth screamed again, and Sean placed his hand over Garth's mouth to silence him. He walked backwards from the goat head, pulling Garth with him, but not turning from the image. As they backed into the safer area of the garage, the goat head pulled back. Sean saw the eyes of the goat go black as it disappeared from view behind the junk pile. The light in the garage dimmed and went out, leaving only the dark and the smell of baked wood.

"Where'd it go?" Garth asked.

"Back into the pile," Sean said.

"What was it?" Garth asked.

"I don't know."

"Do you think it lives in there?"

Sean didn't know, but he was tired of Garth's questions. "Come on, let's sneak downstairs and go to bed. We can come back out here tomorrow and check on it again, see if it's still here."

"OK," Garth said, turning to go with Sean. As they approached the threshold, Garth turned and said, "Thanks for the food!"

Suddenly they heard the sound of a baby crying behind them. Sean and Garth turned to look back at the junk pile. There was the face again. It was the face of an infant, crying and carrying on the way babies do. As they watched it changed into the face of a boy their age, who smiled at them.

"Come back if he's bad again," the face said. "I have more food."

They both nodded and turned to leave the garage.

Six

Garth paused. He took another bite of his bagel and chewed. The waiter came by to check on them, and Garth's entire cup of coffee had gone cold, so he asked for a replacement.

"We would visit the boy occasionally when we were hungry," Garth said. "He wasn't always there. When he did appear, we would try to engage him, find out his name, why he was in the junk pile. He would never say anything more than 'I'm just a baby' or words to that effect. And after my experience with the goat head I never had the courage to explore more of the pile. We were still scared of that area of the garage, we just went there when our stomachs were growling."

Steven was listening intently to Garth. He had a million questions, but he didn't want to interrupt Garth's narrative and make him forget anything.

"There was only one person we ever told about the boy," Garth continued. "That was Davy, who lived across the street from us. He was a little older than us and would play with us in our backyard when Frank wasn't around. For some reason Frank hated Davy, and if he caught us playing with him he'd kick Davy out of the yard and give us a tanning. But we liked Davy a great deal, and we'd play with him whenever we thought we could get away with it.

"Davy was over one day when Sean and I went into the garage for food. He saw the boy. He went right up to the junk pile and grabbed the hand sticking out, held onto it for several minutes. Sean and I were too scared of the boy to ever do anything like that, but Davy wasn't afraid of him at all. They seemed to have some kind of rapport, as though they were communicating on some level that Sean and I didn't know about. I remember asking Davy about the boy, and Davy told us that the boy hated Frank too. Not because he knew him, but because of what he was doing to us. It felt like the boy was our ally against Frank, and Davy could communicate with him."

Garth stopped to take a sip of his warmed coffee and placed the mug back down on the table.

"You're probably wondering what all of this has to do with Frank attacking you," Garth said.

"I think it's incredibly interesting," Steven said. "Please don't edit yourself on my account. I'd like to hear it all, everything you remember."

"All right," Garth said. "I'll continue. Things went on like this for a while, but Frank became more and more abusive. We would escape to the backyard, Davy's house, or the garage to get away from Frank, who didn't seem to care where we were as long as it wasn't around Davy. We wouldn't tell him where we went, and we'd just sneak back into the house at night to go to bed. The kitchen door was always open, because in those days you never locked your doors.

"One day it came to a head. Frank began beating on Sean again, I don't remember why. Any little thing might set him off. Sometimes it seemed he'd do it just to entertain himself. I ran out of the house and hid in the garage, which is what I normally did when Frank was wailing on Sean. When Sean came into the garage after this particular beating, however, I was mortified. Frank had used the belt on him all over his body, including his face, and he had deep red cuts that were bleeding. Sean fell on the ground in the garage and passed out. At first I thought he died, but then I could see he was still breathing. I inspected the damage Frank had inflicted on him, and I was angry. I didn't know what to do about any of it. I knew the cuts needed to be bandaged, but there were no clean bandages in the garage.

"The boy in the junk pile was extending a hand, and I went to it to see if there was food there. I fed Sean what he was able to chew, but he kept passing in and out of consciousness. Gradually he began to improve. Whatever was in that invisible food the boy gave us helped heal some of Sean's injuries; it was miraculous. Eventually Sean was able to sit up. I didn't ask him what had happened because I knew it was painful for him to speak. And it was obvious Frank had beaten the crap out of him.

"I was surprised when the boy called me over. I walked up to the face in the junk pile, and all he said was, 'get Davy.' So I ran across the street and brought Davy back. When he saw Sean he was afraid. The damage was beginning to heal, but Sean was still covered in blood and he looked pretty frightening. Sean was able to talk and he told Davy what had happened with Frank. Frank had beaten him with the buckle end of the belt, which had caused most of the cuts. I remember looking at Davy's eyes as Sean told the story and I saw the same hatred and anger in them that I felt.

"The boy in the junk pile called Davy over and they had a conversation. The arm extending from the pile gave him something, and he returned to us. He told us the boy wanted us to use some items on Frank. He showed us a small object that looked like a wooden matchbox. The other item was a small paper envelope, and inside was some powder. The boy had told Davy we should stop Frank by using the items on him. We asked Davy if the items would kill Frank, and he said no, they would just stop him.

"Sean said he'd do it, so Davy gave him the instructions. The matchbox needed to be placed under Frank's bed, and the powder needed to be placed into something he'd drink. When Frank went to sleep in the bed after drinking the powder, he would pass out. Sean was to cut a piece of his hair and to clip a fingernail from Frank, and bring them back to the boy.

"Sean told Davy he'd do it the next day. Davy said he wanted to be there when Sean gave the hair and nail to the boy, so Sean said he'd call him over when the tasks were done and he had the items from Frank. Davy went home for the night, and Sean and I talked about how he was going to pull it off.

"Sean decided he'd place the matchbox under Frank's bed that night, since Frank would likely be passed out already. He planned to sneak upstairs in the middle of the night into Frank's room, and leave the matchbox. I asked him how he planned on getting the powder into something Frank would drink. We thought maybe we'd try his coffee, since he always took a thermos of coffee with him to the farm in the morning, and we could put the powder into the thermos overnight, and he'd fill it in the morning. But we couldn't risk him rinsing the thermos out before he poured the coffee into it. We weren't sure if we lost the powder or somehow wasted it if the boy would give us more. We wanted to make sure it worked the first time.

"We settled on putting it into his booze, since Frank drinking his whiskey was as predictable as the sunrise. The problem with that plan was that Frank tended to bring a bottle home with him from work, and he'd polish off the bottle that night. There weren't bottles of whiskey lying around.

"We solved that problem by borrowing a bottle from Davy's father. It was the same kind of whiskey that Frank drank, and there was an inch in the bottom of the bottle, so we hoped Davy's dad wouldn't miss it. Sean dumped the powder into the bottle and snuck upstairs one night to place the bottle somewhere Frank would run into it the next day. We were betting that in his drunken stupor he'd never remember whether or not he'd finished last night's bottle before he passed out, and that he'd polish off the remaining whiskey once he discovered it.

"The next day and night Sean and I were on pins and needles, wondering if our plan would work. Would he find the bottle and drink it? Or would he just drink the new bottle he brought home every day?"

◊

Sean and Garth were lying in bed. It was just after midnight. Neither boy had heard sounds from upstairs for over an hour, and Garth was telling Sean he should head upstairs to collect the hair and fingernails.

"Easy for you to say," Sean told Garth. "You're not going up to do it."

"I will if you want," Garth said. "You cut his hair, I'll cut a fingernail."

"No, I'll work the scissors," Sean said. "You might stab him and wake him up."

"How will we know if he's really passed out?" Garth said. "If he wakes up and finds us in his room, he'll be mad as hell."

"He snores," Sean said. "I'll be sure he's snoring before we start. You just stand watch while I clip him, whisper to me if he wakes up."

Garth nodded. The two boys crawled out of the bed and slipped upstairs in their bedclothes. They avoided all floorboards known to creak. It was a warm evening and Frank had a fan going in his bedroom. Its sound helped mask their movements.

Sean tip-toed to the bed and listened for Frank snoring. In the darkness of the room he could see Frank's chest rising and falling slowly, the careful measured breathing of sleep. He glanced to the bedside table where Sean had left the whiskey that he'd dosed with the powder. The bottle was empty. He turned to Garth. Once their eyes met, Sean nodded, and Garth knew they were in the clear.

Sean leaned over the bed and held the scissors up to Frank's head. He squeezed the scissors slowly so they wouldn't close all the way. He took only a few strands of hair so that Frank wouldn't notice when he woke up. Then he moved to Frank's hands.

Frank was lying on his right hand, but his left was free and dangling. Sean moved the scissors down to the hand lying about six inches off the mattress, hanging towards the floor. He inspected each finger in the dim light, looking for one nail that he could cut. They all appeared to be short, too short to clip. The longest nail was on Frank's little finger. He might be able to cut it, but he wasn't sure. He raised the scissors into position and tried to slide the edge of the nail against the blades.

Before he could squeeze the scissor's handles he heard a creak from the base of the bed, and Sean looked up at Garth. Garth was frozen in fear. He'd taken a step back from the bed and the floorboard under him had let out a loud squeak. Frank roused.

Sean pulled the scissors back and stayed down low. Frank's hand raised up and flopped up over his body as he turned in bed. Both boys stayed frozen, waiting to see if Frank had been only disturbed or fully awaken. Sean looked up at Garth again. He was petrified and shaking, stifling a frightened whine. Sean held a finger up to his lips, reminding Garth to stay silent.

After a moment, Frank's breathing returned to normal. Sean mouthed the words "don't move" to Garth and Garth quickly nodded his agreement.

Sean resurveyed the landscape. Frank's head was turned away from Sean, and his left hand was now on the other side of the bed, but his right had become exposed. The hand was pressed tightly against the mattress with the fingers spread out, and Sean saw several nails that might work. Sean knew it would be difficult to get the scissors between the nails and the mattress.

He took his time, sliding the blades of the scissors into position under the nails. As the bottom blade slid in, it raised the finger a little from the mattress. He heard Frank's breathing sputter and he quickly removed the blade in case Frank decided to turn again. After a moment Frank quieted again, and Sean reinserted the blade.

He slowly closed the top blade, only wanting a small section of nail to come off. As the blades connected he saw the nail chip free and fall to the mattress. He removed the scissors and placed them in his back pocket.

Frank began to adjust in bed again. The hand slid away and Frank's body was rolling back towards him. He reached forward quickly and picked up the clipped nail, pressing the nail tightly between the flesh pads of his finger and thumb so he wouldn't lose it. He stepped back from Frank and looked at Garth, who was in the same frozen position as before, holding his breath. He nodded towards the door and Garth let the breath out. They slipped out of the room and into the kitchen. When they reached the kitchen door, Sean silently opened it and the two boys crept out into the shadows of the yard.

"Let's take it to the boy now," Sean said. "I don't want to wait."

"OK," Garth agreed, and followed Sean closely.

They walked through the back yard feeling the cool grass under their bare feet. When they reached the garage, Sean went in first and Garth followed. Sean approached the junk pile. Within a few moments, the boy's face appeared and an arm emerged, holding out an open palm.

"Give them to me," the boy said. Sean let the nail drop from his tightly pressed fingers into the boy's palm. He had been pressing so hard the nail had made an indentation in the tip of his finger. Then he reached into his pocket and removed the few strands of hair he'd clipped from Frank's head. The fingers on the palm closed around the items and the arm retreated into the junk pile. The boy's face disappeared from view. For a moment, Sean and Garth began to wonder if anything more would happen. They waited patiently and after a few seconds the boy's face reappeared and the arm reemerged from the junk pile. It was holding a small watch, about the size of a quarter. The straps of the watch were gone. Sean picked up the watch from the palm and looked at it. The numbers on it were strange, not numbers he was used to seeing on clocks. There was only one hand on the watch.

"Place it in the box," the boy said. The arm once again retreated into the junk pile and the face disappeared, leaving the boys to themselves in the garage.

"The box?" Garth asked.

"The matchbox," Sean said. "The one I put under the bed last night."

"You mean we have to go back in there?" Garth asked.

"Only I will go back in," Sean said. "You nearly gave us away. You go back down to bed, and I'll come down as soon as I've placed this in the matchbox."

"OK," Garth said, and began walking out of the garage and back to the house. Once inside the door they parted ways, Garth heading down the stairs to their bedroom and Sean continuing into the kitchen. "Be careful," Garth whispered as Sean turned to leave him.

"I will," Sean said, "but don't make any noise when you go down the stairs."

"I won't," Garth said, taking his first step down to the basement.

Sean traced his previous path through the kitchen and living room and into the hallway and Frank's bedroom. As he entered Frank's room he kept low to the floor, moving towards the spot under the bed where he'd hidden the matchbox.

He found it and opened it. He reached into his pocket and removed the watch, then carefully placed it inside the matchbox. Then he replaced the matchbox where he'd found it, next to a pair of shoes.

Something seemed wrong. He listened, straining his ears. He couldn't hear anything.

I should be hearing him snoring, or breathing, Sean thought.

He heard the sound of the toilet flushing in the hallway bathroom. Frank was walking back into the room.

Sean slid under the bed and held his breath. He couldn't fit all of the way under the bed. As long as Frank didn't look down as he returned, he'd be fine and he could wait until Frank fell asleep and then leave the room. He heard the feet approaching. He angled his head so he could see the feet.

They stopped at the bed. Sean expected to see the feet turn, hear the mattress groan above him and then see the feet rise up into the bed, but they didn't. They just stood there.

He's caught me, Sean thought, still holding his breath.

He felt the hand wrap around his shirt and pull. He was yanked from under the bed. He felt the wooden slat of the bed frame scrape against his back and arm as Frank lifted him by his shirt.

"Always a thief!" Frank said, slurring his words. He held Sean by the back of his shirt. Sean struggled to get out of the shirt, but Frank was gripping it too tightly. Frank sensed the attempt to escape and brought his other hand down hard against Sean's face. Sean felt the room spinning and felt as though he would pass out.

"Gonna teach you a lesson," Frank said, wobbling on his feet. Sean wondered how Frank had the balance to make it to the bathroom and back. He also wondered how long before the boy's object took effect and the promise of stopping Frank engaged. He didn't know how it would work, but he'd done everything the boy had asked, and right now its engagement was his only salvation from Frank.

Frank slapped him again hard, and Sean tasted blood. A ring on Frank's hand had hit his eyebrow and he could feel something warm dripping down into his eye, blurring his vision, making the dim images of the room dark red. He pulled down inside the shirt Frank was holding, hoping his wiggling would somehow set him free, but he couldn't get his arms out of the shirt.

"Now you'll pay!" Frank said, lifting him higher and shaking him. He pulled back his hand again and brought it down hard on Sean's head. The force of it twisted Sean's head hard to the right and he felt some of the blood on his face go flying to the floor. He couldn't see anything through his left eye anymore. Frank pulled back again and hit him in the stomach. Sean felt all of the air leave his lungs and the blood enter his open mouth as he tried to suck in air.

Why isn't it stopping him? Sean wondered. *Please, stop him! He's so drunk he'll kill me.*

Sean thought about the matchbox. Had he placed it in the right place? Yes, it was under the bed, right where it had been before Frank drank the powder.

Under the bed, Sean thought. *Maybe the bed has something to do with it.*

Frank was winding his hand back for another slap. Sean shifted his feet and instead of trying to pull away from Frank he pushed into him. Frank lost his balance and fell sideways onto the bed.

Sean was pulled down onto the bed with Frank, but Frank wasn't moving. He wondered if he'd passed out. Sean wiggled his shirt free from Frank's hands and stepped away from the bed.

Frank was lying with his face to the side towards Sean. His eyes were open but his body was still. It was as though his body was paralyzed. Sean fought to suck in a breath and finally his lungs cooperated with him. He took several deep breaths, feeling a pain in his side each time he did. Frank still hadn't moved. He wiped the blood from his eyes and moved up towards Frank to look more closely at Frank's face. Frank's eyes just stared, unable to do anything.

Sean poked at Frank, trying to get him to respond. Nothing worked. He slapped his face. No response.

Sean turned on the bedroom light and thought about what to do. He decided to run to the basement stairwell and call for Garth.

Garth came up the stairs and followed Sean into the bedroom. Once he entered the lit room he saw the damage to Sean's face. "Are you all right?" he asked.

Sean nodded.

Garth approached Frank tentatively.

"Is he dead?" Garth asked.

"No," Sean said. "He's breathing. His eyes are open. He just can't move."

"Do you think he can hear us?" Garth asked, still afraid Frank might reanimate and turn on them.

"I don't know," Sean said. "Here, help me get him back into bed."

The two boys maneuvered Frank's legs up onto the bed and positioned him normally. Frank's body was limp, dead weight. Occasionally Frank's eyes would settle on one of them and give them a disquieting moment, but they became bolder with each minute that passed.

"What do we do now?" Garth asked, staring at Frank who was lying still on the bed.

"I guess we go to bed," Sean said. "Let's see how he looks in the morning."

◊

Garth took another sip of coffee. The waiter showed up to remove their dishes, and Steven and Daniel took the moment to lean back in their chairs after having been on the edge of them for the past several minutes.

"The next day he was the same," Garth said. "Comatose. Just staring into space. Couldn't move or do anything other than open his eyes and breathe. Didn't eat, went to the bathroom in the bed. We explained it all to Davy and then decided we'd better tell Davy's mom. We told her that Frank had been in bed all day and couldn't move, and we were afraid something was wrong with him. Of course we didn't tell her what we'd done.

"She didn't relish the idea of coming over to the house with us to check on him, since Frank was a terrible neighbor, but she had seen the look of worry on our faces and decided she'd better check it out. Once she saw him she called a doctor. The next thing you know, Frank was in an asylum and Sean and I were sent off to live in a foster home. It wasn't great, but it was an awful lot better than living with Frank, let me tell you."

Garth paused. He took a long sip of coffee and then sighed, as though he'd just freed himself of a terrible secret.

"You already know Frank died in the asylum years ago. Sean passed away from cancer. I never married, no kids of my own, and now I'm here. But gentlemen, I've still got some fight left in me. If Frank has found a way back, I'll do whatever I can to help you fight that terrible son of a bitch. I'm not as afraid of him now as I was back then."

Steven and Daniel looked at each other. Daniel spoke first.

"I think what you created was a soul cage," Daniel said. "It sounds to me like it was designed to last for eighty years."

"But why come after me?" Steven asked. "No offense Garth, but you'd think his target would be you."

"True," Garth said. "I've not seen Frank in the manner you describe. Maybe he's been visiting me here and I've slept through it. Or, maybe he's targeting you because you have the gift, like Davy had."

Steven looked up at Garth. He'd not told Garth anything about his abilities.

"Yes, Mr. Hall," Garth said, "I can tell. I could see it in Davy, the way he could communicate with the boy, and I can see it in you. In fact, you look a lot like him."

Garth stared at Steven, pinching his eyes a little. Then his eyes went wide, and he set his coffee mug down on the table.

"How daft of me," Garth said. "Of course."

"Of course?" Steven asked. "What?"

"Davy," Garth said. "And you. What was your grandfather's name, Steven?"

"Blair on my mother's side," Steven said, "and David on my father's."

"Davy's last name," Garth said, "was Hall. I believe it was your grandfather who helped us imprison Frank."

Everyone sat quietly around the coffee table, letting this revelation sink in.

"How would Frank know Davy was involved?" Steven asked.

"Depends on the soul cage," Daniel said. "Frank's body was useless, but his soul could continue to observe things, learn things."

"Did you ever discuss this with David…Davy after it happened?" Steven asked Garth.

"Oh yes," Garth said. "Davy had asked us for the details, and both Sean and I told him everything that had played out. Davy was as delighted in Frank's situation as we were, but we were also afraid we'd done something terrible. All three of us went back to the boy in the garage to ask him what had happened to Frank. Davy did all of the communicating with the boy, interpreting the answers the boy gave so we could understand. He never mentioned anything about the soul cage expiring, just said that Frank was alive, was fine, and wouldn't ever bother us again. Sean and I were taken from the home almost immediately after that – we never went into the garage again. I saw Davy once more at a high school dance. He was dating a girl from our school. I remember we talked briefly about Frank. I told him Frank was still in an institution, and I remember Davy saying, 'good, good.' Then our conversation shifted to girls and how to score some beer after the dance. Never saw him again after that."

"Steven, is your grandfather still alive?" Daniel asked.

"No," Steven said, "he died years ago."

"My guess," Daniel said, "is that when Frank's soul was caged, he was angry, in a rage. That's never gone away. He holds Sean, Garth, and David accountable. No offense intended, but Garth is elderly and without children. David, on the other hand, has living children who continue to use the gift. It doesn't surprise me he'd try to exact vengeance there."

"He always hated Davy," Garth said. "Never knew why. He hated him more than he disliked Sean and I. If he learned that Davy was involved in this, I'm sure he'd be furious at him."

"So that means," Steven said, "that in addition to myself, Roy might be at risk. And my son, Jason."

"I'd say so, yes," Daniel said. "It's worth finding out if either of them have been having bad dreams lately."

"What exactly can Frank do?" Steven asked. "He's a ghost, right? Roy and I have fought ghosts before. They can be dealt with."

"Really?" Garth said. "Fascinating."

"I'm no expert on soul cages," Daniel said, "but I do know a little. Frank isn't a normal ghost. A normal ghost occurs after death, when a person goes through death with their body and soul together. When Frank's soul was caged back in 1933, his body became like a shell, operating on automatic. Eventually the shell died. But the soul never died, never went through death, where a conversion takes place. Frank's soul still has a lot of life's power in it. How much, we don't know. We don't know the original terms of the binding."

"When I saw Frank at my house," Steven said, "he was in some kind of glass casing that was restricting his movements."

"That's a physical representation of the cage," Daniel said. "It has stopped his soul from returning to his body, and from doing or going anywhere else for that matter. But his mind is still inside that cage, active, able to gather information in real time. Do you remember when he touched your neck?"

"Yes," Steven said, "the bruising, the way it was moving my skin around."

Garth sat back in his chair, overwhelmed by the discussion.

"Frank certainly didn't have that ability when he went into the cage," Daniel said. "He picked up some skills along the way."

"The cage wouldn't stop him from learning?" Steven asked. "Or from gathering abilities or tools?"

"It would depend upon the tools," Daniel said, "and the terms of the binding. Some tools are purely non-temporal, so if he was determined enough he could have used the last eighty years to prepare for when he'd be released. This isn't a ghost you're dealing with – it's much more lethal."

They both paused and looked up at Garth.

"Gentlemen," Garth said, "I'm sorry this has come down on you. I really am. When we did it all those years ago we had no idea what would happen. We just did it to be free of the beatings. But I will tell you this, Mr. Hall. Sean and I were grateful to Davy back when it happened, for helping us do it. I'm still grateful to this day. I'll be eternally grateful. What Davy helped us do changed our miserable childhoods into something tolerable. I know he felt he was doing the right thing. I think he still would have helped us even if he knew the consequences. But I'm sorry this wheel has turned. I hope you are able to solve it, and if there's anything I can do to help, I will."

"Thank you, Garth," Steven said. "You've been very helpful already. I think Daniel and I will return to Seattle. My father should be returning from a trip today and he might have some ideas on how we can deal with this. I should also check up on my son."

Garth rose slowly to his feet. "Old bones stand up a little slower than they used to," he said. He extended a hand to Steven and Daniel.

"Is the best way to reach you the number here at the reception office?" Steven asked.

"Oh no," Garth said. "Let me give you my cell number."

They exchanged contact information, plugging each other's numbers into their respective cell phones.

"Please let me know how things go," Garth said. "In a way I feel responsible for this mess, and if there's something I can do to help resolve it, I will."

"Thanks, Garth," Steven said. "I'll stay in touch. In the meantime, please don't worry. My father Roy will know how to deal with this; we'll come up with something."

Garth followed them out to the main doors of the facility, and watched them go down the front ramp and towards the parking lot. *I wonder what Sean will think of this,* he thought, turning to walk to his room.

Seven

On the drive back to Seattle, Steven replayed the meeting with Garth in his mind. He was searching for any clue Garth might have mentioned that could lead them in a particular direction. He was coming up empty. He grew frustrated at the idea this problem was something from the past, something his progenitors didn't take care of. Now it fell to him to figure it out, and he was feeling resentful.

"There's got to be something we can do," Steven said. "It seems to me like we're running out of time. I'm just guessing here, but I get the feeling Frank will be harder to kill when he's free of the cage."

"Yes," Daniel said, "he'll be easier to deal with while he's in the cage."

Steven paused. "Don't take this the wrong way Daniel, but 'deal with' isn't what I have in mind. Frank's body died years ago, and his soul had its hand wrapped around my neck recently. Hearing Garth's story, I mean to extinguish the guy."

"Oh," Daniel paused. "Killing him is certainly an option from my perspective. Just using an euphemism."

Steven simmered on the idea for a few moments, steeling his resolve. This would not end like Michael or Jurgen, with life still left in them, problems still waiting to happen. Frank had threatened him directly and he would find a way to eliminate Frank completely.

"Any ideas on how to kill him while he's still in the cage?" Steven said.

"Well," Daniel said, "the problem is the cage itself. Without knowing the original terms of the binding, we don't know what type it is and what can get in or out. If we can find that out, we might be able to figure out what vulnerabilities there are and come up with something that would work."

"To kill him," Steven said.

"Yes, to kill him," Daniel said a little uncomfortably.

"And if he gets out before we kill him?" Steven asked.

"You're right, it's going to be more difficult if he gets out. There will be other options if he's free of the cage, but he'll be much more dangerous. If we can figure out how to do it while he's still in the cage, that would be best."

"And by 'do it,' you mean 'kill him,' right?" Steven asked.

"Yes," Daniel said, a little irritated.

"It seems it's a word you're not very comfortable with," Steven said.

"I don't think you should ever be comfortable killing anyone or anything," Daniel said. "It should be uncomfortable."

Steven decided to let the subject drop for now. He let the discussion bounce back and forth in his mind instead. Roy should be home by the time they reached Seattle, and he wanted to talk about David with him. He remembered Roy convincing him to not pursue Michael even though he'd been involved in some horrific child murders. He remembered him and Roy leaving Jurgen twisting in pain in his office after removing his powers; why didn't they just kill him? He deserved it. So did Michael. Leaving these horrible people alive just gave them a chance to recover and pursue more evil. Even the Manitou had left Jurgen alive. People with the gift seemed to have a real reticence to kill, even when it seemed appropriate or necessary. Maybe it was some code. *Like the ten commandments,* Steven thought. *Thou shalt not kill.* But that was in a normal world where you couldn't live forever or trap souls. What exactly are the rules in the world of ghosts?

"Pardon me for just a moment," he said to Daniel. He pulled out his cell phone and scrolled through the names, looking for Jason. He found it and hit dial. He hated others who used cell phones while driving but this couldn't wait.

He reached Jason's voicemail. "Jason, this is Dad. Would you give me a call when you get this message? It's important. Thanks."

He returned his phone to his pocket.

"Does Jason know?" Daniel asked.

"About Frank? That's what I hope to find out," answered Steven.

"No, I meant about the gift," Daniel said.

"Oh," Steven said. "No. He doesn't. At least as far as I know."

"Do you think he has it?"

"What, the gift?"

"Yes."

"To be honest with you I hadn't really thought about it."

"I see. Best to just keep him out of this?"

"Well yes, to the extent he can be."

"That's how I feel about Troy," Daniel said, "though it's Eliza's decision, of course. I suppose it's the natural desire to protect your children. But if it turns out he has the gift, I struggle with how appropriate it is to deny him the knowledge to develop it. I mean, if you found out your kid had some special skill, like he was a really good baseball player, you would encourage him to play little league, right? You wouldn't pretend little league doesn't exist, or worse, bar him from playing it? That would seem cruel."

"I suppose so," Steven said. "Hadn't thought of it that way."

"The gift is like being a prodigy in some ways," Daniel said. "They take prodigies out of grade school and put them in college courses so they can advance. Leaving them in elementary schools just stunts them, frustrates them."

"I'm confused," Steven said. "So you would or you wouldn't teach Troy how to develop his gift?"

"I'm saying I struggle with that," Daniel said. "If he even has it. Eliza doesn't tell me much about him. But I do wonder."

"Last time I saw him, his interest seemed to rest squarely in video games."

Daniel smiled. "I sent him that Xbox. Eliza was pissed but she let him keep it. She told him she won it in a contest."

"I hope I'm not betraying a confidence, but she told me she doesn't know when she'll tell Troy."

"That doesn't surprise me. Sounds like she's right where I am. Thanks for telling me. I'll keep that bit of information to myself."

"We're getting close to my father's place," Steven said. "Do you mind if we swing by and see if he's returned from his trip?"

"Not at all," Daniel said.

"No job to get back to?" Steven asked.

"I'm a writer," Daniel said. "I can make anything work."

◊

Roy looked a little sunburnt.

"How was the trip?" Steven asked.

"Relaxing as hell," Roy said. "Dixon knows how to kick back, let me tell you. He's perfected the act of relaxation to an art."

"Glad to hear it," Steven said. "This is Daniel. He's been helping me while you've been gone."

Roy and Daniel shook hands. "Helping him, are you?" Roy asked. "Sounds like something's up. Well, follow me into the kitchen and you can tell me about it. I have a few things to unpack."

They both followed Roy. Steven took a seat at the kitchen table and motioned for Daniel to sit as well. Roy began unpacking several plastic bags. He pulled out a beautiful large shell and handed it to Steven.

"Look at this!" Roy said. "An animal lived in that thing. Dixon hit the shell like this," he grabbed the shell back to demonstrate, "and the thing crawled out. Dixon stabbed it and we barbequed it for dinner. Delicious." He handed the shell back. "Beautiful, right?"

"It's a conch," Steven said, turning the shell in his hand.

"I don't remember what the hell Dixon called it," Roy said. "And look at this!" He pulled two large bottles of dark liquid out of the bags. "Local rum! Want a taste?"

"Later, Dad," Steven said. "Listen, I want to hear all about the trip but we need to talk to you."

"What's up?" Roy asked, still pulling items out of bags and placing them on the counter.

"Your father, David, pissed off a man eighty years ago by imprisoning him in a soul cage. Now he's getting out and coming after me. After us."

Roy stopped emptying the bags and stood still, staring at the kitchen cabinets. He didn't turn to look at Steven.

"Frank Wilmon," Roy said, his enthusiasm gone. "Am I right?"

"How'd you know?" Steven said.

Roy returned to unpacking the bags. "My father wrote about him in his book. One of the first things I was ever able to read in that book, because he told me all about him. Frank was one of the first times my father used his gift. He was afraid of Frank and wanted me to know about him."

"And you never thought to tell me?" Steven said.

"It didn't seem relevant," Roy said. "Just a story my dad told me."

"Well, that story had his hand around my neck the other night," Steven said. "He threatened to kill me. With you gone I needed some help, and Eliza referred me to Daniel here. He and I tracked down one of Frank's kids, an old man named Garth. He lives in Olympia. We just came from there. He told us the whole story."

"Why don't you take a deep breath," Roy said, continuing to unpack, "and start from the top. Tell me everything that's gone on."

Steven and Daniel relayed the entire story, starting with Steven's first visit from Frank through all the details of Garth's experiences.

"You'd think Frank would start with you instead of me," Steven said, "being David's son."

"I was out on the water," Roy said. "That's why he couldn't reach me. What about Jason?"

"I have a call out to him, waiting to hear back."

"So you're an expert on time, Daniel?" Roy asked.

"Well, I do know something about it. I've studied it over the years," Daniel said.

"What do you think?" Roy asked him.

"Well," Daniel said, "I think it's very dangerous. The cage is definitely collapsing. I figure there's 48 hours left before he's completely free. And he's picked up some skills while he's been in there. Steven's skin was undulating and twisting where Frank had grabbed him. His touch left some residual power that was very disturbing. It might have been very small-scale time shifting on a molecular level."

"Time shifting?" Roy asked.

"The cells of the skin each moving backward and forward in time, by just a split second. It would make it appear that it was moving when viewed in normal linear time."

"Sounds bizarre," Roy said.

"It's dangerous. It's hard enough for a human to handle a shift in time if your whole body is involved. What he did caused a piece of Steven to be out of sync with the rest of him. If he could cause that effect on a wider area, say on a vital organ like your heart or your brain, it would probably kill you."

Daniel paused. "In fact, that might be the technique of the soul cage. That might be how his soul was removed from him. He might have found a way to use the same power that entrapped him."

"So the cage might not be expiring," Steven said, "he might be destroying it from within?"

"Maybe," Daniel said. "Impossible to know for sure without more information on the cage itself."

"I like this guy," Roy said to Steven, nodding toward Daniel. "He knows his shit. And any friend of Eliza's is a friend of mine."

"He's been invaluable," Steven said. "Without you here I was kind of lost."

"We need to talk to that face in the junk pile," Roy said. "That's our next move. We need to know where the garage is."

"I can call Garth," Steven said. At that moment Steven's cell phone rang. He looked at the display.

"It's Jason, let me take this," he said, rising and walking into the other room. Roy and Daniel listened to half of the conversation but couldn't tell what was going on.

Steven returned from the other room. "Jason is at my house, waiting for me to get home. Daniel, can you make contact with Garth and find out the location of that garage? I'm going to go over to my house and talk with Jason."

"I'll come with you," Roy said.

"No, I want to talk to him alone," Steven said. "Daniel, are you up for going with us to visit the garage?"

"Absolutely," Daniel said, "if you want me along."

"I do," Steven said. "Dad, can Daniel stay here with you while I go do this? I'm not sure where the conversation with Jason will go but I want to do this on my own."

"Sure," Roy said. "He can stay."

"And Dad," Steven said, "can I take all the protection you've got sitting around? I'm going to ask Jason to take some."

"Sure, let me round it up," Roy said, turning towards a cabinet.

"Would that device you gave me work with Jason?" Steven asked Daniel.

"Yes, it should," Daniel said. "Same instructions I gave you. Don't let it get taken away. You have to keep it close. I can give you another one – I have several in my backpack in the car."

"What about the protection you gave me? Any more of that?" Steven asked.

"I think your father's protection is probably stronger than mine," Daniel said. "I'd use that."

Roy returned with two large Mason jars filled with a clear liquid. "I made a ton when we were dealing with Jurgen," he said. He handed them to Steven.

"Thanks. Would you mind whipping up some more for you and me? We're going to need it too."

"Sure, I can make more while you're gone."

"Can I watch?" Daniel asked.

"Of course not," Roy said. "My father told me to never show anyone how it's made, except when I pass it along to Steven here. Family secret."

"Daniel tells me it's pretty potent," Steven said. "He analyzed it in his lab in Spokane."

"More variants than I've ever seen," Daniel said.

"One of my father's obsessions was this protection," Roy said. "He inherited the recipe from his dad, of course, but he refined it for years, modifying it, making it stronger. Gave me his recipe just before he died. I've been making it exactly the same way since then."

"I'm leaving to go meet Jason," Steven said. "I'll be back as soon as I can."

Steven took the two Mason jars and left.

◊

When Steven saw Jason, he was immediately concerned. Jason was just an inch shorter than him, but thinner and more muscular. He had blonde hair, blue eyes, and a dimpled chin that drove girls crazy. Jason had always been a good kid, a mother's boy, kind to everyone and everyone liked him back. His success in soccer helped him with a scholarship to the university and he always seemed healthy and fit. Not today.

Steven inspected the bruises on Jason's neck. At first he thought they might be hickeys but upon closer inspection he could see they went all the way around his neck, even to the back. Jason was clearing his throat often and seemed run down and tired.

"Tell me what happened," Steven said.

Jason shifted from foot to foot while his dad continued inspecting his neck. "I thought someone was playing a prank," he said. "I was dreaming I couldn't breathe. I woke up and found this. I thought maybe one of my roommates had snuck in and strangled me as a joke."

"This is no joke," Steven said. "Does it hurt?"

"Yes," Jason said, "every time I swallow, and when I turn my head to the extreme right or left."

Standing behind Jason, Steven surreptitiously dropped into the flow and watched the bruises for any unusual sign, any shifting of the skin that might mimic the strange movement he'd seen on his own skin. There didn't appear to be any. He exited the flow quickly. The effect had disappeared on his own skin after a short while following the attack, so it might have already passed on Jason too.

"You don't remember anything? Any one in the room with you? A man? Glass?"

"Glass?" Jason said. "What are you talking about?"

"I've had the same problem, the last three nights. My sleep has been disturbed. But I woke up to see what it was, while it was happening. I was attacked." Steven pulled his collar down to show Jason the bruising on his neck. "I believe the same person attacked you."

"What?" Jason said. "How can that be? Who?"

"The who and the why are long stories that aren't relevant at the moment. The main thing to know is that you, I, and your grandfather, Roy, are all under attack."

"Under attack? What are you talking about?" Jason was looking at Steven funny, concerned that his father had gone off his rocker.

"Let me put it this way," Steven said, stopping to take a breath. "An ancestor of ours committed a crime against this man, or so he thinks, and he's exacting revenge by coming after Roy, myself, and you. Roy and I are working on a way to stop him. Until we do, this is a dangerous threat, and I believe our lives are at risk. I'm going to need you to do a few things to protect yourself."

"I've already got a shotgun, Dad," Jason said.

Like grandfather, like son, Steven thought.

"A shotgun won't work on this guy," Steven said. "You'll need to do a few other things."

"What kind of guy won't a shotgun work on?" Jason asked.

How far do I go? Steven thought. *Do I tell him exactly what this guy is?*

"You're going to have to trust me," Steven said. "A shotgun isn't going to work."

Jason turned his head skeptically towards Steven. He knew his father had never been a big fan of guns. Steven saw the skepticism.

"Believe me," Steven said, "if I thought a shotgun would work, I would have already tried it. I wouldn't hesitate to use it."

"I wonder if Grandpa Roy would feel the same way," Jason said, aware that Steven's father was a gun enthusiast.

"I've talked with your grandpa about it. He agrees with me."

Jason didn't look convinced, but Steven continued anyway.

"Both he and I need you to protect yourself with some things I'm going to give you. The first is this," Steven said, pointing to the two Mason jars on the table between them. "Listen to me and follow my instructions exactly. I want you to swallow two big mouthfuls of this just before you go to bed. Set your alarm for four hours and get up and take another two mouthfuls. You got that?"

"What's it do?" Jason asked, eyeing the containers.

"It's going to make it harder for this guy to touch you, to harm your neck," Steven said.

Jason didn't respond. He continued to look skeptically at the jars.

"The other thing," Steven said, retrieving the rectangular object from his pocket, "is this. I want you to wrap this against your arm using Ace bandages while you're sleeping. It's important that it be close to your body and in a place where no one can take it from you, like your roommates. Please don't show it to them. No one should know about it or the liquid, either. They're the only things standing between you and this guy until I and your grandpa can figure out how to deal with him."

Steven caught himself using the same euphemism he'd criticized Daniel for using. *Didn't want to use the work 'kill' in front of your own son?* he asked himself.

Jason looked at his father. "What's going on?" he asked. "This isn't you. I know you. You don't believe in this kind of voodoo shit. Grandpa maybe, but not you."

'Grandpa maybe?' Steven thought. *What does Jason already know about Roy?*

"Would it make you happier if you heard it from your grandpa?" Steven said. "We can call him. He'll tell you the same thing."

"No," Jason said. "We don't need to call him. I want to know why *you* are telling me this. This isn't you."

Do I tell him now? Steven wondered. *This could go off rails so easily. I'd rather tell him when we're not in the middle of a crisis.* Steven decided to punt.

"I need to get back to Roy's and work with him on this, try to get it solved," he said. "The main thing I need to know is that you'll do as I've asked. Keep the object safe and on you with the bandage, and drink the protection."

Whoops, Steven thought. *Wonder if he'll catch that.*

"Sure, I'll do it," Jason said, "on one condition."

"What's that?"

"When you get it figured out with grandpa, you both tell me what was really going on. The whole story."

Steven knew he couldn't lie to his son if he agreed. Jason wanting to know seemed the element he was most worried about. Since Jason had put this option on the table he decided to take it.

"Yes," Steven said, "we'll do that."

"OK then," Jason said. "I'm going back to my apartment." He slipped the rectangular object into his coat pocket and looked at the Mason jars.

"Do not let anyone else drink that," Steven said. "It may taste like booze but trust me it's far more than that, and it's difficult to come by."

"I won't," Jason said. "I'll hide it from my roommates."

"Come here," Steven said, extending his arms. Jason rolled his eyes but let his father wrap him in a big hug. "I love you and want you to be safe. Make sure you do as I've said."

"I will," Jason said. Once Steven released him, he took the Mason jars and headed for the door.

Eight

Steven pulled the car up to the address Daniel had obtained from Garth. He, Roy, and Daniel stared out, looking for the garage of Garth's story. It was nowhere to be seen.

In its place was a small strip mall with a couple of businesses. Next door was a church.

"Well, it's been eighty years," Steven said. "What were the odds it would still be here?"

"Looks like they weren't good," Roy said. "I expect the boy was forced to move, and he probably didn't want to move far. Ghosts never do if they can help it. Can you figure out exactly where the garage might have stood?"

Steven scanned the strip mall for numbers. "The number on this salon on the end is the same number Garth gave me. So there's a good chance it's sitting where the house used to be."

"Based on the story from Garth," Daniel said, "the garage would be maybe fifty feet from where the house stood."

"That would place it either in that pizzeria," Roy said, "in the church, or in whatever is behind the salon."

"I'll see if there's an alley," Steven said, moving the car. They circled the block, checking the spot from all angles.

"Nothing behind but asphalt," Daniel said. "It's either the pizzeria or the church."

"My money's on the church," Roy said, "but I *am* hungry."

Steven parked the car and the three walked into the pizzeria and took a booth. A friendly waitress with an exaggerated lilt to her voice took their order and they discussed their plan.

"Let's scan the whole place, wander around," Roy said. "Look for anything that might seem unusual. I'm going to guess the boy, if he's still here, likes to live under things, so look for piles of stuff."

One by one they rose from the table and walked around, checking out the rest of the restaurant, the restrooms, the back exit, and a janitorial closet. Roy stuck his head into the kitchen. The others could hear him talking with the kitchen staff.

Reconvening at the table, Daniel and Steven waited for Roy to return.

"Is he on a bathroom break?" Daniel asked.

"I expect he's trancing in there," Steven said. "I'm not exactly sure how we're supposed to figure out where this ghost might be from just visual clues. For all we know from just looking around, he might be haunting this booth. A trance might help narrow things down."

The food arrived as Roy returned. The men chowed down on the pizza.

"Well?" Steven said between bites.

"Not here," Roy said. "But the church is a good possibility. Something's in the basement there."

Steven paused eating for a moment so he could enter the flow. He rose from the table and hovered over the restaurant. He could see nothing. Then he moved over to the church. He couldn't see anything there either. He left the River.

"You must have tranced to figure that out," Steven told Roy. "I can't see anything in the flow."

"I did," Roy said. "And it's well camouflaged. That boy does not want to be found."

"We'll need to be in physical proximity of him to interact with him," Steven said, remembering his experience with Roy in Oregon. It was easier to detect ghosts while in a trance, and sometimes one could see them from within the River, but they would only respond if you were physically there with them.

"Let's finish this pizza and go over there, see how the land lies," Roy said.

Roy took one more bite and was up and out of the booth, leaving Daniel and Steven to take care of the rest of the food and the bill.

"He moves quickly, doesn't he?" Daniel said, smiling. "Barrels right in."

"He's the old man and half the time I have trouble keeping up with him," Steven said. "Be prepared to just go along with whatever story he might concoct."

They rose and left the restaurant, leaving some cash at the table. As they turned to walk toward the church they saw Roy already halfway there, headed for the back of the building. By the time they reached the front of the church, Roy had already scoped out the building's exterior and met them at the entrance.

"Two exits in the back if we need to break in," Roy said.

"Why don't we try just walking in the front door first?" Steven asked.

"Just planning ahead," Roy said, smiling. They walked up a short flight of stairs and opened the door to the church.

It was dark inside. The entryway opened up into a chapel with rows of pews. In the distance on a dais there was an altar and an organ. Light shone into the chapel at the far right, where an open door let fluorescent light stream in. "An office," Roy said. "Let's try there. Follow my lead."

They walked through the dark chapel and towards the open office door. As they approached it Steven could see metal desks and filing cabinets. Inside was a small woman, rotund, with black hair and very vivid makeup.

"Hello?" Roy said as he entered.

"Oh, hello," came the reply from the woman, rising from her desk and walking towards Roy. "How can I help you?"

"My name is Hill and these are my associates, Mr. Youngman and Mr. Smith," Roy told her, pointing out Steven and Daniel respectively. *At least he left the 'Henny' out this time,* Steven thought.

"Pleased to meet all of you," the woman said politely.

"I'm writing a book on historical churches in the area, and these are my assistants on the project," Roy said.

"Oh, how wonderful!" the woman replied.

"You are?" Roy asked.

"Mrs. Peterson. Judith," she said. "Are you interested in our church?"

"Well, yes, I am," Roy said. "It looks to me like it might have a history that would be appropriate for my book. But I have to tell you, I couldn't find out much about it on the internet. So I thought I'd come down and visit and see if someone might be able to help me learn more about it, to see if it's right for the book."

"Oh, I'm sure the pastor would love to have our church in your book," she said. "Membership has been on the decline I'm afraid, and anything that might help bring in more parishioners would be very helpful."

"Well, that's fantastic," Roy said. "You'd be surprised how some churches don't want to cooperate to the extent that's necessary in order to be written about in a detailed historical account." Roy gave her a big smile. "When was the church built?"

"Nineteen forty-eight, just after the war," she said. "Before that, this was just a residential area, and before that, farmland. We've had twenty-two pastors here since it was built. Jeremy Wayne is our current pastor."

"Would he be available for an interview sometime?" Roy asked.

"It would be a while," Judith replied. "He's currently in Africa on a mission. We have an assistant pastor who's giving the Sunday services, but as I said there's not many church members right now so the pews are pretty empty on Sundays."

"Why so few members?" Roy asked. "This looks like a beautiful church."

"That's the question we ask ourselves every day," Judith said. "We've tried everything over the years."

"So it's been a problem for a while?" Roy asked.

"Oh yes, this church has struggled for as long as I've known it," she said. "It wouldn't surprise me if it's struggled since it was built. I donate my time to keep the office in order for Pastor Wayne since he is such a caring and thoughtful man, truly doing the Lord's work. But keeping the church going has been difficult."

"I wonder if the church has records of membership?" Roy asked. "From the past? That I might examine for the book?"

"Well, yes we do," Judith said. "And I'd be happy to let you examine them, but..."

She looked worried. "Yes?" Roy prompted her.

"...but they're down in the basement and I'm afraid I don't have access to that area."

Steven watched the wheels in Roy's mind turning.

"Oh, it's blocked off or something?" Roy said.

"Locked up," she said. "Pastor Wayne has the only key. He left instructions to not go into the basement without him." She gave an uncomfortable laugh. "To be honest with you, that's perfectly fine with me. I've been in the basement twice, and it's a little creepy."

"I wonder what information about the history of the church would be down there as opposed to up here, where we might peruse it?" Roy asked.

"Most of it is down there," she said. "So I suppose what I can do is take your number and have Pastor Wayne give you a call when he returns, so he can set an appointment with you to access it."

"When does he get back?" Roy asked.

"Next month, around the 20th. I'll make sure he calls you."

"Tell you what," Roy said, "that should work out fine. I'm planning on being back in the area at the end of next month, and I'll stop back in and see if he's available. You've been very helpful, Judith. I think your little church here might make a wonderful addition to my book."

Judith blushed a little, although it was hard to tell under the makeup. "Well, I'm delighted to help. I'll tell Pastor Wayne you stopped by once he gets back. I'm sure he'll be excited to participate."

Roy turned to leave, and Steven and Daniel followed suit. They walked back through the dark chapel, and as they left through the main doors, they heard Judith say, "thanks again."

The door closed behind them. Roy turned to Steven and Daniel. "We'll jimmy the back door. There's no alarm system."

They waited until it was dark. They chose a door that wasn't facing the street and was partially hidden by a tree and shrubs, intended only as an emergency exit. It led to a short hallway behind the dais. Steven used a flashlight to navigate to the end of the hall where there was a door secured with a padlock.

"Great, now what?" Daniel said.

Roy placed the crowbar behind the hinge holding the lock and pried the hinge out of the door. It left holes where the screws had been.

"They're going to know who broke in," Steven said. "It'll be obvious, we were just here asking about the basement."

Roy produced a bottle of wood glue. "We're going to glue it back in place. She's too scared of here to come check anything before the pastor returns. By the time he gets back, this glue will have set it back in place."

Steven seemed skeptical but the deed was already done. Roy turned the handle and the door opened to a wooden staircase that descended into darkness.

"Here we go, boys," Roy said. Steven shone the flashlight down the steps and started down.

It was obvious the basement hadn't seen visitors in a while. Cobwebs were plentiful. It was half finished with wooden floorboards and walls. Steven found a pull cord to turn on a bare bulb overhead. The room was thick with dust.

"Let's try to not stir up any more of this dust than we have to," Steven said, shining the flashlight into the rooms beyond.

"Any idea where the boy is?" Daniel asked.

"No, I just know he's down here," Roy said.

They moved from area to area. Most were filled with banker's boxes, presumably filled with documents. There were old wooden filing cabinets in some sections. One area had large boxes filled with Christmas decorations. Eventually they worked their way back to the furthest corner, where several boxes had been stacked haphazardly. They looked very old and fragile, as though lifting them up might cause them to dissolve. It looked as though no one had touched them in many years.

"Here," Roy said, pointing to the boxes.

Steven shined his flashlight on the boxes. They were stacked in a way that created gaps between them. Some of the gaps were small, others were larger, several inches wide. It looked dark inside the gaps.

"Do we wait?" Daniel said.

"No," Roy replied. "I'm going to go into a trance. Let me see if I can get him to manifest."

"You usually sit for this," Steven said, looking around for a chair but finding none.

"I'll just stand this time," Roy said, removing his blindfold from his pocket. He handed it to Steven, who wrapped it around Roy's head. "Keep an eye on me," Roy said.

Steven stepped back from Roy and turned off the flashlight. There was very little light in the basement and he couldn't see Roy at all. He decided to turn the flashlight back on but keep it concealed in his pocket; that created just enough light so he could watch Roy. While Roy was in a trance it was Steven's job to make sure he didn't hurt himself.

The creepiness of the basement began to seep into Steven as he stood next to Roy, waiting for Roy to make contact with the boy. The ceiling was low, almost to his head, and it felt claustrophobic. The half-finished wooden walls allowed images from other areas, and it felt as though he was being watched from between the wooden planks. He understood why Judith didn't want to come down here.

After several minutes Roy began to breathe more deeply. Steven glanced at Daniel, and saw that he was in the River. He felt a little jealous, like he'd been left with the boring job no one wanted to do. Still, Roy had to be watched. Dangerous things had happened to him while he was in a trance, and Steven wasn't about to let his father wander and fall, or step into something sharp.

Roy emerged from the trance and removed his blindfold. Daniel opened his eyes at about the same time.

"He's afraid of adults," Roy said. "But he's willing to talk to us. Daniel should do the talking."

"Why Daniel?" Steven asked.

"Because I have a son about his age," Daniel said, "and I think he might be a fellow time enthusiast."

Daniel approached the boxes. "Steven, could you let a little more light into the room?" he asked.

Steven removed his flashlight from his pocket and shined it into a corner at the other end of the room. The boxes and the dark gaps between them became more visible.

Daniel scanned the boxes, looking for the boy. Steven saw the face appear in one of the gaps and stifled a gasp. It looked like it was just behind the box, dimly lit, and greyish white. As he watched, it changed from the face of a toddler to a ten year old.

"Hello, Sam," Daniel said.

"You know my name?" the boy said.

"Yes, and do you know mine?"

"No," the boy said. His eyes moved around the room.

"I'm Daniel. And this is Roy, and Steven. They're friends. We're all friends."

The face of the boy shifted to several years younger, a five-year-old. He didn't reply to Daniel.

"Sam, we're here because of Garth," Daniel said. "Do you remember Garth? And Sean, and Frank?"

"Yes," Sam said. "Frank used to beat them."

"That's right," Daniel said. "And you helped Sean and Garth stop Frank, do you remember?"

"Yes, I remember," Sam said. "And Davy."

"Yes," Daniel said, "Davy was Roy's father. And Steven here is Roy's son."

"Oh," Sam said, "fathers who let their sons live. Why?"

"All fathers want their sons to grow old," Roy said.

"Not all fathers," Sam said. "Not my father." Sam's face began to shift rapidly between ages. When he would speak, the face would normally be a ten year old. When he wasn't speaking it would drift between a toddler and a five or six year old. The constant morphing was jarring and Steven found it difficult to concentrate on the words the child spoke.

"Your father didn't want you to grow old?" Daniel asked.

"No," the boy replied. "Because my mother didn't. I failed her. He told me so."

"What happened to you, Sam?" Daniel asked.

"I got older. I wasn't supposed to. I disappointed her."

"Everyone gets older, Sam. You can't control it."

"She said I could. She said if only I could have remained a baby, things would have been perfect. I tried to stay a baby. But I kept getting bigger. She was so sad."

"Your mother wanted you to never grow up?" Daniel asked him.

"Yes," the boy said. "I tried, I really did."

"What happened, Sam?" Daniel asked.

"My father. She was so sad and upset, he knew he had to do something to make her happy again. He loved her very much. So he tied me to the bench in the garage."

Sam paused.

"What did your father do?" Daniel asked.

"He hit my head with a hammer."

Steven felt the air going out of him and sadness and anger rise in the back of his throat.

"I remember thinking as he hit me, if I could just become younger, mother would be happy again, and father wouldn't have to do this. I tried to become younger as he hit me, so he would stop. But it didn't work. When he was done, he buried me in the forest."

"All boys grow up," Daniel said with a frog in his throat. He was clearly shaken by the boy's story. "What your father did to you was wrong."

"No," Sam said insistently, "he loved my mother. He needed to make her happy. It was my fault."

Daniel felt it best to move on rather than risk angering the boy. "When you helped Garth and Sean, you gave them things. A wooden box and a powder. Where did you get these things?"

"Martha's friends."

"Who's Martha?"

"Martha moved into my house after my mother and father moved out. I loved Martha."

"Martha knew about you? Out in the garage?"

"Oh yes, she could see me and hear me and understand me. Like Davy. Like you."

"Martha would talk with you?"

"Yes, once she found out I was in the garage, she would visit me all the time. She wanted to help me. She helped me become younger."

"How did she do that?"

"Her friends. People like you stayed with her all the time. There were always people in the house. She introduced some of them to me. They helped me too."

"How did they help you?"

"They taught me things. They taught me how to do this." Sam's face switched rapidly from an adolescent to a baby and back again. "See? I'm younger now. If I could only find my mother, I'm sure she'd be happy again."

"So Martha's friends taught you how to shift yourself?"

"Yes. Martha couldn't do it, but her friends could."

"What else did they teach you?"

"They taught me how to protect myself. I know how to scare people."

Steven thought of the goat's head that Garth described.

"So if people try to disturb you," Daniel asked, "you scare them away?"

"Yes," the boy said. "It usually works. It didn't work when they tore down the garage. But I just waited, and eventually I found this place. No one bothers me here. Except Jeremy."

"Jeremy visits you here?"

"I love Jeremy. He's like you, and Davy."

So Pastor Wayne has the gift, Steven thought. *No wonder he keeps this place locked up, he's protecting the boy.*

"Sam, you said that Martha's friends gave you the objects you gave to Sean and Garth," Daniel said.

"Yes, they did," the boy answered. "The ones I gave to Sean and Garth I got from William. He was a very nice man. He taught me many things about how to be younger. One day he told me he had to leave in a hurry, and he wanted me to have his things. He gave me a large bag full of objects. I never saw him again. I've been playing with them, figuring them out. Some of them I know how to use, like the ones I gave to Sean and Garth. Others I have no idea how they work."

This is right up Daniel's alley, Steven thought.

"The ones you gave to Sean and Garth, we need to know more about those," Daniel said. "Frank's soul was trapped by them, but the cage is coming loose. Frank will be free again soon. He plans to attack Roy and Steven, and Steven's son Jason, to punish them for what Sean and Garth did, because Davy helped them."

"Is Frank going to kill them because they're too old?" Sam asked.

"No," Daniel answered, "because Roy's father, Davy, helped imprison his soul all those years ago. Davy followed your instructions. He told Sean and Garth what to do, remember? Now Frank wants vengeance. He's angry, like when he used to drink and hit Sean."

"He made Sean go hungry," Sam said. "He was a bad man."

The child's illogic was swirling in Steven's mind. It was OK to murder someone for being too old, as his father had done to him, but not OK to starve them. *Ghosts are truly fucked up*, Steven thought. *Just as Roy told me.*

"We need to understand the cage," Daniel said. "Frank is still in the cage, even though it is coming loose. We need to stop him before he can get out of it. We only have a few hours to do something to stop him."

"I have more of them," the boy said. "I could give you another one. You could do it again."

"Frank's body died years ago," Daniel said. "There's no way to get him to drink anything."

"You could try this," the boy said. As they watched, a thin, frail arm extended from another dark gap in the boxes. Its tiny hand held a wooden box with intricate carvings, about twice as large as a pack of cigarettes.

Daniel reached for it, but stopped. "What is it?"

"They're bugs," the boy said. "Jeremy gave them to me. He brought them back from one of his trips. He gave me several boxes, so he won't mind me giving you this one."

"What do they do?"

"They can crawl inside him. He won't be able to figure out where you are. Don't open it until you're ready. They can only live for a few seconds outside the box without someone to go in."

Daniel took the box. "Thank you, Sam, that's very kind of you to share with me."

"Here," said the boy, extending his arm again. On his palm were a couple of small objects. "Take these too."

"What are they?"

"I don't know. William gave them to me. Maybe you can figure them out."

Daniel looked like he'd just won the lottery.

"Will you come back and visit me again?" he asked.

"I will, if you want me to," Daniel said.

"Yes, I would like you to," the boy said.

"Jeremy may not let me in, though. He keeps this place locked up."

"I'll ask Jeremy to let you in," the boy said. "He's very nice. I'm sure he'll let you visit."

Steven's concern heightened. He wasn't at all sure it was a good idea for Sam to tell the Pastor that he'd had visitors. Then again, there was no way to stop him from telling the Pastor anyway.

"Do you want us to find your body, in the forest?" Daniel asked. "We could bury you properly in a grave. Maybe a hallowed grave, here at Jeremy's church?"

"No," the boy said. "Please don't. I want to keep trying to get younger. If I could just stay younger long enough, mother will love me again."

"All right, we're going to go now, Sam," Daniel said. "Thank you for visiting with me. I'll try to come back and see you later."

"Goodbye," the boy said, his face beginning to dim.

Nine

"I've only heard about these," Daniel said, "and most people think they're a myth."

They were in the car, returning to Seattle. Daniel was in the back seat, looking at the wooden box that contained the bugs.

"What do they do, exactly?" Roy asked.

"Well, if I marry up what Sam told me," Daniel said, "with what I've heard about them, they're a kind of parasite. The box keeps them dormant. When I dump them out they'll seek a host."

"So the idea would be to dump them out onto Frank, if he appears tonight?" Steven asked.

"Yes," Daniel said. "One of the side effects of these insects is that they open up all moments in time, but they cause the host to misjudge the present moment. It creates constant anxiety in the host that they feed off. That will neutralize Frank, because he'll never be able to find us."

"What, he'll be looking for us for eternity?" Roy said.

"Essentially," Daniel said. "He'll have billions and billions of moments to choose from. The odds of him picking our present moment are so great, he's effectively gone forever."

"I would prefer to kill him," Steven said. "Leaving him hunting for us for the rest of time seems like a bad idea."

"It works," said Roy. "It achieves the goal."

"No Dad," Steven said, "my goal is not to leave another monster able to return and cause havoc. We left Michael, we left Jurgen. David left Frank. Nobody ever finishes up these problems, they just 'neutralize' them. Frank needs to be gone, not just inconvenienced in his search for us."

"I don't think you fully understand what 'gone' means," Roy said. "Nothing's ever really gone. Frank's body is dead, but you can't kill a soul, not one with this kind of energy."

"And these things," Daniel said, examining the other objects Sam had given him while not really paying attention to Steven and Roy's discussion, "are amazing. One of them might be a rare chronosphere. I'll have to check it back in Spokane. Absolutely amazing, can't believe he gave them to me."

"Sam likes you," Roy said. "I think the fact that you've got a boy that is about his age when he died made a connection with him that neither Steven or I would have been able to make. So I'm glad you came along."

Steven was still fuming from the kill vs. neutralize conversation. He'd go along with the plan for now, lacking any better alternatives. But if an opportunity arose to completely take down Frank, he was going to do it.

◊

They all decided a large room was needed to work in, so Steven decided to sleep on the couch in the living room. Roy and Daniel agreed to watch, taking shifts if necessary. Steven removed the rectangular object from his arm and left it in his bedroom, locked in a nightstand drawer. He didn't drink any protection. This time they wanted Frank to appear.

"The moment we learn Frank is in the room," Daniel said, "we should move into position around Steven."

"Then you'll open the box?" Roy said.

"Yes, I'm guessing he'll grab Steven by the throat, that's what he's done in the past. I'll move over to him and open it. Be prepared to enter the flow immediately after I do; I don't think you'll be able to see these insects unless you're in the River. We only need one to enter Frank. If there are a couple more, they'll die off quickly, but don't touch them."

"What about the glass?" Steven said. "Will that stop them from entering him?"

"It shouldn't," Daniel said. "The cage keeps him from getting out, but it shouldn't stop things from getting in."

They settled into chairs and Steven rested on the couch, closing his eyes. It was just after ten o'clock and they were all tired from a long day.

"Daniel," Roy said, "perhaps you and I should drink some protection."

Before Daniel could answer, the glass figure appeared in the room. It was not standing next to Steven, it was standing next to Roy. In two quick moves, it had its hand around Roy's neck, then had Roy lifted off the couch.

"Steven!" Daniel shouted, waking him. Steven swung his feet off the couch and stood, moving over to Roy and the glass figure. Roy was gasping for air.

Daniel stood and raised the wooden box above the left shoulder of the figure. He slid the lid of the box open, and turned the box upside down. At first Steven saw nothing come out, then he remember to enter the River.

Once in the flow, he looked for the insects. There were not one or two emerging from the box, there were *dozens*. They were bright white and about four inches long. They twisted back and forth as they moved, like a centipede. Several landed on the glass surface of the figure and began to bore into Frank. Dozens more hit the ground and began to slither around, searching for a host. Steven saw a couple remain on the box, and began twisting towards Daniel, who was still holding it.

Drop the box! Steven thought. Daniel didn't move. He wasn't yet in the flow.

Steven left the flow at the exact moment that Daniel entered it. He rushed behind Daniel and swatted the box out of his hand. It crashed to the floor and slid a few feet away. Then Steven reentered the flow.

Several of the centipedes had made it to Daniel's hand before the box was dropped, and were crawling up his arm. Daniel could see them now and was swatting at them.

The glass man had dropped Roy, who was holding his neck in pain. Roy had entered the flow, and was avoiding the insects as they moved toward him. They were slowing.

Vertical bars began to appear in the glass man and within a few seconds he was gone. Steven turned to look at Daniel, who was still struggling with the insects. He had swatted all of them off his arm except one, which he was pulling on. Its head had entered the skin near his wrist, and Daniel had hold of the body of the insect, tugging at it.

Help me, Daniel thought. Steven didn't know what to do to help.

Just hold onto it, Steven thought. *Don't pull so hard you break it.*

It's boring into me, Daniel thought. *It's got its head in already. I'm not pulling it, I'm just trying to hold it in place. It's going to break itself off. Do something! Hurry!*

What do we do? Steven thought. The idea of using a flame to get a tick head to release from the skin came to mind, but would that work on these creatures?

It didn't matter. Steven saw the body of the insect snap, leaving an inch of the body in Daniel's fingers. Before Daniel could drop the broken half and reach for what was left of the bug, it slithered under his skin. Daniel looked up at Steven, panicked.

Maybe we can cut it out, Steven thought.

Vertical bars began to appear in Daniel, and he started to fade.

Daniel! Steven thought. *Wait!*

In another moment, Daniel was gone. All of the white centipedes on the floor were now still, turning translucent. Steven exited the flow.

Daniel's body was slumped on the floor.

"Shit!" Steven said, kneeling next to Daniel and searching for a pulse. It was there, he was still breathing.

Roy returned from the River, holding his neck, barely able to speak. "What happened to him?" he asked.

"One of them got into him," Steven said. "He didn't drop the box fast enough. Hundreds of those bugs came out, there were too many of them."

"Some landed on Frank?" Roy asked, kneeling next to Daniel's body.

"Yes, that part worked, I think," Steven said. "What do we do?"

"Help me get him up onto the couch," Roy said. They lifted Daniel carefully and laid him down. He seemed to be sleeping.

"Well, this is fucked up worse than Hogan's billy goat," Roy said.

"Do we take him to the hospital?" Steven said. "We know what's happened to him, but we certainly can't tell the doctors and nurses that."

"We gotta get this figured out," Roy said, "or he'll stay like that forever. And if he's in a hospital, it'll make it damn hard to do anything with him when we have a solution."

"I'll call Eliza," Steven said. "Maybe she'll know what to do."

"Yes, call her," Roy said.

Steven took out his cell phone and called her.

"Steven?" Eliza answered.

"Eliza? We've got a big problem."

◊

Steven saw Eliza waving her arm at the arrivals pick up. She was hard to miss. She was a tall and imposing woman, but not overweight. Her hair was wild, swirling around her head chaotically. She moved gracefully and deliberately. She had a large suitcase with her. Steven parked the car at the curb and popped the trunk, then stepped out to give her a big hug and help get the suitcase into the back of the car. They both hopped back into the front seats and Steven drove out of the airport. It was around 10 a.m. Eliza had taken the first flight out of Sacramento.

"It was bad timing," Steven said. "Had he entered the flow just a second or two earlier he would have seen how quickly the insects were moving and how many there were."

"I found this medical supply store on the internet," Eliza said, referring to an address she had on a scrap of paper. "It's between the airport and your home. I need to stop there and pick up some things on the way to your place if that's all right."

"I'm sorry, Eliza," Steven said. "This was certainly not how I wanted your first visit here to go. And I'm sorry I got Daniel wrapped up in this."

"Daniel's a big boy, he makes his own decisions," she said.

"But Troy…" Steven said and then paused, unsure if he should have brought it up.

"Ah, he told you," Eliza said. "Well, that does complicate things. But I'd be helping him no matter what, he's a good friend."

"You found Troy a babysitter?"

"He's staying with Joe. Having Tommy to play with, he'll think he's in heaven. So he's fine. And Joe will keep an eye on the barrier."

"Any ideas how to proceed?" Steven said. "Roy felt we shouldn't take him to a hospital."

"God no," Eliza said. "They'd just poke at him and it'd make it hard for us to do what we need to do. No, his body is going to need some routine care but we can do that. We'll get an IV going to keep him hydrated, and we may need to place a tube in him to feed him. I'll catheter him and we'll get a bedpan. We'll keep him clean and comfortable, make sure he doesn't get bedsores or his muscles atrophy. It's a short term solution but we can keep his body going for a while. Unfortunately, just as we need a time expert, we've lost access to the best one I know."

Steven reached over and grabbed Eliza's hand. "I know we'll figure this out," he said.

She squeezed his hand and looked back at him. "I'm not so sure."

◊

When they arrived at Steven's house, Roy was there. He and Eliza greeted each other warmly and they took Eliza to Daniel. He'd been moved into the guest bedroom next to Steven's room. Steven half expected Eliza to react when she saw Daniel lying on the bed like a corpse, but she went straight to work without a moment's hesitation. She checked all of his vital signs, then began arranging things, asking Steven for help as she went. After an hour she had Daniel's room the way she wanted, and she joined Steven and Roy in the living room. Roy had his book in his hands, reading through it. Steven was sipping coffee.

"Would you like some?" he offered to Eliza.

"I would love some," she said. Steven went to the kitchen and poured her a mug. *I think she takes it black,* Steven thought.

"Correct," she said from the other room. Steven smiled and brought the mug to her.

"Well, he's about as comfortable as I can make him," she said, sipping at the hot coffee and settling into a stuffed chair. "I can guarantee you this was the right thing to do. The hospital wouldn't have known what to do with him, and they'd just be sending him through endless tests trying to figure it out. Daniel doesn't have that kind of money. As long as we keep an eye on his fluids, he should be fine for a while."

"Any progress with the book, Dad?" Steven asked Roy.

"Some," he said, "some. Turns out Charles knew a bit about parasites. He didn't call them that, but that's essentially what they are."

"What does he say?" Eliza asked.

"Well," Roy said, "he had a drawing here that looks an awful lot like the buggers Daniel used." Roy twisted the book around and showed the picture to Eliza and Steven. It did indeed look like the white centipedes that had emerged from the box. It was difficult to tell scale from the drawing.

"He lists a lot of different parasites and what they do. He's noted that this one is rare, so there's not much about it, but there's several pages about other ones. Some of them are quite nasty."

Steven shivered, thinking of one of the insects burrowing under his skin. It was the stuff of nightmares.

"The good news is that there is a common method to remove these parasites that seems to work on all – or most – of them."

"What is it?" Steven asked.

"It's a salve that you rub on the body. The recipe for it is here. Once the salve is applied, the afflicted party drinks a special type of protection. That recipe is here, too. According to this, once they drink the protection with the salve applied, the insects leave the body."

"Well, that might work to get the bugs out," Eliza said, "but it won't solve the problem. In fact it might make it worse."

"How so?" Steven asked.

"Well," she said, "these parasites open up all moments in time, and then confuse him as to which one is our present moment, right?"

"That's what Daniel said they would do," Steven answered.

"Then Daniel is off in one of a billion different moments. When you remove the parasites, he'll lose his ability to move to different moments. He'll be stuck in whatever moment he's in when you remove them."

Roy and Steven looked at each other. It seemed plausible.

"We've got to bring him back to our present moment," Eliza said, "*then* remove the parasites. Any other way and you've just trapped him in oblivion for the rest of his life."

"And another problem," Roy said, "is that he's comatose. He can't drink anything."

"I can inject it down his feeding tube," Eliza said. "Once it hits his stomach, it'll be as though he drank it."

"OK," Steven said, "let's suppose we have him all salved up and we're ready to go with the protection. All we need to do is find a way to bring him into the present, and once he's here, Eliza shoots the protection down his gullet. The insects emerge and he recovers. The only thing we need is a way to bring him to the present."

"What would pull him back from wherever he is?" Eliza asked. "There must be a way."

"Let me keep scouring the book," Roy said. "I'll start looking for something time-related, things about other dimensions, the present tense, that kind of thing. See if something turns up."

"Can either of you think of anyone who might have ideas about this?" Steven asked. "Someone else with some expertise that we might be able to bring in to help? What about the directory, Roy?"

"I'll check it," Roy said. Roy flipped to the section of his book that listed out the various people he and his progenitors had come across over the years.

"Unfortunately, Daniel was the best time man I know," Eliza said.

"What about Dixon?" he asked Roy.

"Dixon's specialty is patterns, not time," Roy said.

"Albert?" Steven asked.

"I don't mind trying Albert if we can't find something on our own," Roy said. "He'll charge to hook us up."

"Isn't it worth paying?" Steven said. "Daniel's life is on the line here."

"Oh, I don't mind paying," Roy said. "It's not that. I don't know how much Eliza might have in savings, but I guarantee you Albert would cost us more than you and I have combined, son."

"Why don't we go about getting the materials we'll need for the salve and the protection," Eliza said, "and think more on this. Let Roy have some time with the book. Something might emerge."

"All right," Steven said, not entirely sure he was willing to drop the possibility of using Albert.

"Roy, will you transcribe out those two recipes?" Eliza asked. "We can get started on them."

Roy turned back to the pages on parasites and asked Steven for a pen and pad of paper. When he was done he looked over the list.

"The protection recipe is simple enough," he said. "Ingredients are all common. In fact I think my own protection would probably work, but let's make this up as directed in order to be sure." He handed the list to Eliza, who looked it over approvingly.

"This recipe for the salve, though, will be a little more challenging," he said. "All the ingredients are easy enough, except one: ghost matter. I don't have any, never have. Do you Eliza?"

"No," she said. "Never cared to have it around. Too volatile."

"Jurgen dealt in ghost matter," Steven said. "Maybe…"

"No way," Roy said. "I'll go collect it from a ghost myself before I deal with that ratfuck again."

"Well," Eliza said, "that might be what we'll have to do. Go collect it. Anyone know a place where we can get ghost matter?"

Steven, Eliza and Roy all smiled at each other. It was a light moment in an otherwise rough day.

"I'll go," Steven said. "Eliza, you're the only one who knows how to keep Daniel going, will you stay here with him?"

Eliza nodded. "I'll call Claire and ask her to meet you at Mason Manor. If you want her along, that is."

"I would love to have her help," Steven said. "Dad, will you stay and keep working on the present moment problem? Even if I bring back some ghost matter, it won't do us any good if we can't figure out how to pull Daniel back to us."

"I'm on it," Roy said.

"By the way," Steven asked them, "do either of you know how to collect ghost matter?"

Ten

Steven was an hour outside of Salem when he got the call from Roy.

"It's good news," Roy said. "I think we have a method to bring him back to the present."

"That's great!" Steven said. "What is it?"

"Well, it's rather extreme. And it'll change things for Daniel, permanently. But it might save him."

"Tell me what it is, Dad."

Roy sighed. "The book calls it a fusing. It's like a possession. I ran across it entirely by accident, since being in the present is just a side effect of it. If we fuse another soul to Daniel's, his soul will be returned to the present for the process. We'll be able to drive the parasites out while that's happening."

"Fuse a soul?" Steven asked. "What's the impact to Daniel of that?"

"He'll be possessed, so to speak. His body will host two souls, his own, and the fused one."

"Any way to un-fuse it once it's done?" Steven asked.

"Not that I've found," Roy said. "I think it's a one-way ticket."

Steven thought about this. Daniel was unable to voice his opinion in the matter. Perhaps it was something Daniel could live with, even find valuable to his studies. Then again it might make him miserable for the rest of his life.

"What does Eliza think?" Steven asked.

"She's for it," Roy said. "Anything is better than the state he's in now."

"I can think of some states that might be worse," Steven said. "We'd better fuse the right soul; he's going to be stuck with them for a long time. How do you even find a soul for this?"

"Ghosts are candidates," Roy said. "They're usually sticking around for a reason. I thought I'd try Sam, see if he'd agree to it. They seemed to have a rapport and have common interests. I'm going up there today and talk to him, present the idea to him."

"It's worth a shot," Steven said. "How does it work once we've got a candidate?"

"Too long to explain over the phone. This is long distance. I'll tell you when you're back. Good luck down there."

Steven didn't want to get into an argument with his father over flat rate mobile phone calls. Roy had grown up in an era when every minute on a phone was expensive, and old habits die hard. He let it drop.

"I'll let you know how it goes," Steven said, and hung up.

◊

The stretch south of Portland seemed endless to Steven. When he finally pulled up to Mason Manor, it was close to 10 p.m. He recognized Claire's Volkswagen in the parking lot. Claire was a friend of Eliza's who lived nearby. She had helped Pete and Sarah deal with the ghosts in the manor before.

The rest of the parking lot was full; the place must be packed. He smiled as he walked to the entryway.

Pete and Sarah met him at the door. Pete took Steven's bag from his shoulder and placed it on his own. Steven and Roy had helped Pete and Sarah rid their establishment of an invader that was killing their guests, and in the process had come to discover that the manor was thoroughly haunted. The ghosts became a tourist attraction, and Pete and Sarah's business had been saved from bankruptcy. When Steven called, asking if he and Claire might get rooms for the night and do a little exploring in the manor's basement, Pete and Sarah immediately agreed.

"Steven, come in," said Sarah. "We were just visiting with Claire in the sitting room."

They walked into a beautifully furnished room adjacent to the entryway. Claire rose from a loveseat and walked over to Steven, shaking his hand.

"It was good of you to come," Steven said.

"You don't have to twist my arm to get me to visit this place," Claire said, her curls bouncing around her head as she talked. "I love it here."

"The parking lot looks full," Steven said to Pete and Sarah.

"We've been running ninety percent," said Pete, smiling. "Ever since you and Roy solved our little problem."

"I hope Claire and I aren't kicking someone out of their rooms," Steven said.

"No," Sarah said, "we had two left, so it worked out perfectly."

They all sat down in the furniture. "I'll take this along to your room when you're ready to go up to it," Pete told Steven, setting his bag down by the chair he sat in.

"I'm worried," Claire said to Steven. "Eliza didn't sound good on the phone. She said this was quite urgent."

"I'm afraid it is," Steven said. He relayed Daniel's condition to the group, and then backtracked and gave them the whole story. Pete watched him intently as he told the story, looking as though he was witnessing the most riveting movie he had ever experienced.

"I normally wouldn't have anything to do with collecting ghost matter," said Claire, "since I think it's a disgusting practice and very disrespectful to the ghosts. But for Daniel I'm willing to try."

"Is this dangerous?" Pete asked, his voice rising. "It sounds like it might be dangerous."

"I'm hoping we can find a willing ghost," Steven said. "I've never done it before, but I've had the process explained to me. The ghosts here had been harvested before, and they weren't happy about it. I'm hoping we can find one who'll be sympathetic to our cause."

"How do you intend to do it?" Sarah asked.

"The basement," said Steven. "They're plentiful down there. Claire and I will go down, one of us will enter a trance and see if we can communicate with one of them. If we find a willing donor we'll collect the material and I'll be on the road back to Seattle first thing tomorrow morning."

"Steven is making it sound simpler than it is," Claire said. "Few things irritate a ghost more than having its matter removed. Even if they're giving it up willingly, ghosts are very unpredictable and can change their minds on a dime. This will be tricky."

"I'll have to defer to your opinion," Steven said, "since I've never done it before. I just know that if we don't get some, we'll never be able to revive Daniel. He'll be comatose forever, until his body gives out."

Claire looked down at the floor and nodded her head. "We'll find a way to get some," she said. "Somehow."

"Pete," Steven said, "I don't know how long this might take. If you don't mind, I'd like to unpack and then get started with Claire. Hopefully we'll be done quickly, and I'll meet you all for breakfast."

"Of course," Pete said, rising from his chair and grabbing Steven's bag.

"Really, I can carry the bag, Pete," Steven said.

"Are you kidding?" Pete said. "After all you've done for us, you'll never carry a bag in this establishment. I've got your key right here. You're in the north wing."

Steven smiled and turned to Claire. "I'll meet you back here in fifteen minutes? And we'll get started?"

"I'll be here," Claire said.

◊

When Steven saw the room Pete was taking him to, he let out a groan.

"Something wrong?" Pete asked.

"No, it's just this room," Steven said, "I know what happened in it. I met the ghost."

"I'm sorry, Steven, I didn't know," Pete said. "It's the only room left."

"Don't worry, Pete, I'll deal with it," Steven said. "You're doing me a huge favor just putting me up."

"What happened in this room?" Pete said, opening the door with the key and walking inside.

"There's a ghost in here who wanders the room, moaning about a man – her husband, or lover, I don't know – and after she works herself up into a frenzy, she pulls out a revolver and blows her brains out. They hit there," Steven said, pointing to the spot on the wall where he'd seen the apparition's blood splatter.

Pete stared at the spot Steven was pointing at. It looked fine, without a blemish. His face slowly lost color as he imagined the event. "Oh no," he said, "is it going to keep you up all night?"

"No," Steven said, "I doubt I'll see her, unless I go into the River."

"The River?" Pete asked.

Steven sighed. He was tired, and he'd slipped up and said too much.

"It's a way of seeing things differently. A flow of things you don't normally see."

"Oh, your gift," Pete said. "It has to do with your ability."

"Yes," Steven said. "That's how I saw her in the first place. If I don't go into that flow, I probably won't see or hear her at all. It really isn't a problem, Pete. It just creeps me out a little, knowing what she does in here."

"It creeps me out too," Pete said. "That's not one of the stories in *The Ghosts of Mason Manor*. Maybe I should have the author contact you, so we could list it in the next edition."

"Sure, Pete," Steven said, wanting to unpack and get back down to Claire. "Next edition. I'd better get a move on if I'm going to meet Claire."

"Oh yes, here's your key, good luck to the both of you. I've left the basement unlocked. I'll see you both at breakfast in the morning, right? Seven a.m. in the dining room."

"Yes, I remember," Steven said. "Thanks for your help, Pete. See you then."

Pete left the room and closed the door. Steven placed his bag on the bed and removed a thin object wrapped in leather. He tucked it into his back pocket, grabbed a flashlight from his bag, double checked that he had the room key, and left the room to return to Claire.

◊

Steven and Claire descended the stairs into the basement. The manor was silent; all guests had turned in for the night.

"I've met a couple of the ones down here," Steven said, "and they're intense. One was a little girl who killed her parents. The other was a man with an ax."

"Hmm," said Claire. "Neither sounds promising."

"No," Steven said, leading Claire to the spot where Roy had gone into a trance and Steven had seen the portal. "We could use some new ones. How should we do this?" Steven removed the leather pouch from his back pocket.

"Is that it?" Claire asked.

"Yes," Steven said. He unwrapped it. It looked like a wooden tube, about an inch thick. On one side there was a hole in the tube. Next to the hole a rock was worked into the wood. The rock was thick with minerals that looked like crystals.

"Nasty device," Claire said. "I had hoped to never use one."

"I'm thinking maybe the way to do this is for you to conduct the trance, see if you can find a willing donor," Steven said. "Once you find them, I'll collect the matter."

"By scraping them with that blade," Claire said.

"Yes, I believe that's how it's done, based on what Roy told me."

"How will you know if you've collected enough?" Claire asked.

"Roy said if I filled half of this tube we'd have enough."

"Can you imagine if I asked you to fill half that tube with your flesh?" Claire said.

"No, I can't," Steven said. Claire was starting to get on his nerves.

"It's barbaric," Claire said.

"It's for Daniel," Steven said. "Trust me, I wouldn't be down here otherwise."

Claire shot him an unhappy but resigned glance and placed her hands at the side of her head, her fingers touching her temples. Steven realized she was starting her trance. He watched silently as she rubbed the sides of her head as though she had a headache. After a while her head began to tilt, and she abruptly opened her eyes.

"The ghosts here are far too evil to talk to," she said. "None of them are going to help us. Let's try another room."

They walked together to the next room. The basement was a series of open rooms, housing the water heaters and furnaces of the manor. It also held Pete's workshop. They walked up to it, and Claire stopped to try a trance again.

She went through the same routine. After several minutes, she spoke.

"Steven, I think you should see this."

Steven entered the flow and saw Claire in her trance, surrounded by a thin membrane. Claire pointed to a man who was strapped to a wall. As Steven watched, another figure materialized, holding a metal rod. The end of the rod was glowing red, as though it had been resting in a fire. The man brought the glowing rod up to the body of the strapped man and pressed it into his flesh. Steven saw it sink deeply into the man's skin. The strapped man let out an ungodly howl.

"Where'd you bury it?" the man with the rod asked. "You've got a lot of skin left to burn off, Williams, and I've got all night." He raised the glowing end again and held it by the man's face. The strapped man turned his head from the heat, and the man with the rod touched it to the strapped man's ear. It sizzled and turned black under the rod.

Steven turned his head away. *None of these people are going to help us,* he heard Claire think. *They're degenerates.*

Steven exited the flow and Claire came out of her trance.

"We've got to keep trying," Steven said.

"I'll try the whole basement if you want," Claire said, "but I'm not hopeful."

They moved to another area and Claire went into a trance again. She was only in it a minute when she abruptly opened her eyes and began walking into another area.

"What's wrong?" Steven asked.

"A woman," Claire said. "Extremely evil. I can't be around that."

Steven sighed. He didn't know if Claire was telling him the truth or exaggerating. He followed her as she rounded a corner. Steven recognized the area as the spot where he, Pete, and Roy had dug up some gold through a hole in the wall. He shined his flashlight on the wall and couldn't see where the hole had been made. *Admirable patch job,* he thought.

Claire closed her eyes. Once again her hands went up to her temples, and she rubbed. This went on for several minutes before she began to cry.

Steven entered the flow to see what was going on. A young man sat with his back against the wall. He held a long blade in his hands. He was sobbing, occasionally raising his eyes upward as though looking for guidance from above.

He's just lost his little boy, he heard Claire think. *Just a baby.*

As Steven watched, he raised his blade to his throat and ran it across his neck. Blood emerged from the cut and ran down his throat; his sobs stopped. His head fell back against the wall, looking upward.

Let's try him, Steven thought.

He's in pain, he heard Claire think. *You'll just make it worse.*

He's lost someone, Steven thought. *Maybe he'd be willing to save someone else.*

The young man disappeared from view. In a few moments, he reappeared, holding his knife as before, crying into his arms.

"You there," Steven said to the young man.

"What?" the man said, his head still in his arms.

"You've lost your child?" Steven said.

"Yes," he cried. "He's dead."

"What happened to him?" Steven asked.

"He fell," the man said. "And now he won't move. He's not breathing."

"My friend can't move either," Steven said. "He's trapped. And I need your help to save him."

"Leave me alone," the man said.

"Your son is gone, but you can save my friend," Steven said.

"How can I do that?"

Steven removed the matter knife from his back pocket. "By giving me a little bit of yourself," he said, showing the knife to the man.

The man raised his head from his arms and looked at Steven and the knife. "You can go to hell!" he said, lunging at Steven with his blade extended. Steven felt the blade enter him just below the shoulder. He slipped out of the flow.

Claire opened her eyes. "Are you all right?" she asked.

Steven inspected his shoulder. It hurt, but there was no mark, no blood. "That felt real," he said. "I think you may be right. This is going to be more complicated than I thought."

"Don't misjudge the damage," Claire said. "Just because you can't see a wound physically doesn't mean you aren't wounded."

What does that mean? Steven wondered. *The knife wounded me elsewhere? In the flow? Do I believe her?*

"What do we do?" Steven said. "These ghosts are so wrapped up in their own experiences you can't really appeal to them rationally."

"We need one that will work with us, that knows it's a ghost," said Claire. "Think back to the ghosts you met here before. Which of them were cooperative?"

"Well," Steven said, "there was Dennington, in the north wing hallway. Appears only around midnight. He's trying to find his room, and he's been cut or stabbed. And there was a little girl, down here in the basement, who explained what was happening here to Roy. She was the one who had killed her parents. Those two were probably the most cooperative."

"I met the woman in the pantry," Claire said, "and she talks a lot, and remembers people she's met. But I don't think we'd get her to help us until after she goes out to hang her laundry and gets killed. Sarah and I met a met a woman who was…"

Steven turned to look at Claire. She had lost her train of thought, and was looking at the entryway of the room. Steven turned to look at the entryway she was staring at, but saw nothing.

"What is it?" Steven asked.

"He's listening to us," she said. "Over there."

Steven slipped into the flow, but the entryway still appeared to be empty. Then, as he watched, the faint image of a man's head emerged from view on the left, as though he was spying on them. When he made eye contact with Steven, he quickly pulled his head back behind the wall, hiding.

"Hello?" Steven said. "Are you listening to us?"

"Yes," came a faint voice from behind the opening. A tingle crawled up Steven's neck; the man's voice had something wrong with it, and the feeling he got listening to it disturbed him.

"You want some matter, like those harvesters," he said from behind the wall.

"Yes," Steven said. "We do. It's to help save someone's life. Would you be willing to give us some?"

"I would," the man said, still behind the wall. "As long as you're willing to do something for me?"

"What's that?" Steven asked.

"That man leaning against the wall," he said. "The man who stabbed you so viciously. I need to talk to him. I know something important that will stop him from killing himself. It will set him free. But he's too obsessed to listen to me. If you will talk to him, convince him to walk over here to me so I can talk to him, I'll give you some matter."

Steven turned to look at Claire. *It's worth a shot,* Steven thought.

Something's not right, Claire thought.

We've got to get this matter collected somehow, Steven thought. *I don't mind giving it a try.*

Be careful, Clair thought.

"OK, I'll talk to him," Steven said to the man still hiding behind the entryway. "Why don't you come out from there so I can see you? It'll make it easier for him to come over and talk to you."

"No," the man said, "I can't do that. Whenever he sees me he becomes more hysterical. I need you to bring him to me, and help calm him."

Steven turned to look at the man against the wall. He was in the same position he'd been in before he stabbed Steven, crying with his head down on his arms. *How am I going to get this guy to get up and follow me?*

"You there," Steven said.

"Leave me alone," the man said, his head in his arms. Steven could see the knife in his right hand.

"This man can help you," Steven said.

"What man? How can he help me? He's not breathing anymore."

"He can help," Steven said. "Come with me, you'll see."

The man looked up at Steven, tears streaming down his face. "He can bring my boy back?"

Steven didn't know what to say. He just knew he needed the man to get up and follow him to the entryway, so he could talk to the man there.

"Yes, he can help your boy," Steven said, uncomfortable with the lie, but not knowing how else to get the man to move. "He might be able to save him."

A ray of hope flashed across the man's face. "Where is he?" he asked Steven. "If he can help my boy…"

"Over here," Steven said, backing up and turning to the entryway. "Through here."

The man rose from his seated position and stood facing Steven. The knife was still in his right hand, but he didn't seem angry or ready to use it. He stumbled towards Steven and the entryway. As he approached Steven stepped out of his way and pointed to the dark entryway. "There," he told the man, "he's right around the corner."

Steven saw the look of appreciation on the young man's face as he stepped towards the entryway, searching for the man who would help save his son.

The moment he passed the entryway, the man behind the wall descended on him. The man grabbed the young man's head with both hands, holding him still.

Wait! Steven thought. *I've led him to a trap.*

It was too late. The mouth of the man behind the wall opened and rapidly grew until it was a foot in diameter, pushing up and distorting his other facial features. His eyes turned yellow and a row of large fangs appeared inside the lips, which were stretched so far they looked like they would snap. In a quick motion reminiscent of a snake, the transformed man attacked the head of the young man he was holding, snapping three quarters of the head into his mouth. Steven heard Claire scream behind him. The young man swung his arms wildly trying to get free of the creature, the knife cutting through the air, trying to make contact with it. The arms of the creature swiftly changed from human arms to long, bent legs, coated with fine hair. They had crab-like pinchers on the end of them, and in a swift movement one of them shot out and clipped off the young man's hand at the wrist. His hand and the knife fell to the floor.

Steven could hear the young man screaming inside the mouth of the creature, which was pulling the young man's body to the ground. As it descended the creature continued to morph until it looked like a cross between a lizard and a spider. Once it reached the ground, it lunged forward towards the young man's body, taking his head further down its throat. The young man continued to thrash.

What do I do? Steven thought. *How do I help him?*

You can't help him now, Steven heard the creature think. *But you're welcome to take some of his matter while I ingest him. It'll take me several minutes to swallow all of him.*

Steven's mind reeled. He'd just helped feed this man to this creature, and now he was invited to add insult to injury by taking the man's matter against his will.

You wanted the matter, the creature thought. *Take it, your share for helping me.*

I didn't know you intended to kill him, Steven thought.

He's already dead, the creature thought. *I'm merely ending his endless cycle of torment. Doing him a favor, really.*

Looks more like you're eating him, Steven thought.

Well, yes, the creature thought, *that I am. Doesn't mean you can't have some too.*

Steven was disgusted. He turned to look at Claire, who had turned her head away from the scene.

Should I take it? he thought to Claire.

I don't know what to tell you, Claire thought back. *It's up to you.*

Steven saw the creature lunge forward again, its mouth expanding to take the young man's shoulders. The yellow eyes of the creature stared at Steven.

If I take some, Steven thought, *how do I know you won't attack me, too?*

I'm a ghost eater, the creature thought. *Your body stinks. If I were to eat you, I'd be retching for weeks. No chance.*

Why didn't you just come into the room and eat him? Steven thought. *Why'd you wrap me up in your attack?*

There's a barrier here at the door, the creature thought. *Placed here just before his wife killed the child. I've been checking on him for years, the poor bastard, hoping the barrier would dissolve, but it's very strong. Stumbling across you two changed everything. I'm very grateful. Please, take your matter. You earned it.*

Guilt for participating in the trap racked Steven. The idea of taking the young man's matter this way seemed repellent.

The creature lunged again, its fangs rising out of the shoulders of the young man and landing squarely in his mid-back.

You'd better hurry, the creature thought. *The rest goes down rather quickly, and if you're not going to take it, I'm going to.*

The young man had stopped fighting the creature and was lying still on the floor. Steven knelt by the young man's feet and removed the matter knife from his pocket. When he placed his hand on the young man's leg it passed through it, unable to make contact. But when he placed the bottom edge of the matter knife on it, it rested on top of the leg. He pressed and pulled the knife towards him, the bottom blade of the device digging into the young man and scraping off part of him, like a wood plane. Steven raised the knife and saw a small amount of ghost matter inside the tube.

I understand why the ghosts were pissed about this, Steven thought. *This is loathsome.*

He placed the knife back at the man's legs and repeated the procedure, pressing and scraping several times. With each scrape he felt worse. He imagined his own flesh being scraped off in this manner, and it gave him a case of the willies, his body shaking in response. He checked the tube again and saw that it was nearly full. He went down for a couple more scrapes so he could fill it completely. As he finished the last one, the creature lunged again and its mouth took in more of the body, the fangs landing at the young man's knees. Startled, Steven fell backward and quickly exited the flow.

"Let's get out of here," he said to Claire, who nodded and followed him as he walked through the empty entryway towards the basement's stairs.

Eleven

His guilt over how he'd collected the ghost matter far outweighed the concern he had for the ghost in his bedroom, and Steven found it difficult to sleep. Part of him wanted to leave right away and drive all night back to Seattle, but he knew if he tried such a stunt, he'd probably drive into a ditch on the side of the road. He was exhausted and there was no way he could drive eight hours. Eventually the exhaustion overcame him and he fell asleep. The wake up alarm came way too early and he slept through it. When he woke again he found himself late for breakfast. He hurriedly threw on some clothes and headed down to the dining room.

The others were already well into their meal. The table he'd dined at on his previous visits had been reserved for him, Claire, Pete, and Sarah, and it was a good thing, as the rest of the tables in the room were filled.

"Sorry I'm late," he said, pulling out his chair and sitting at the table. "This is a nice change from the last time I was here," he said, motioning to the other tables.

"Thanks to you," Sarah said, passing him a pot of coffee.

"Claire tells us you were successful last night," Pete said. "Down in the basement."

"Yes," Steven said, looking at Claire, who met his gaze but looked away. "I suppose we were. We got the matter, at least."

"Sounds complicated," Sarah said, picking up on the vibe between Claire and Steven.

"Let's put it this way," Claire said, "I hope to never do something like that again."

"It was for a good cause," Steven said. "It will save a man's life. But I have to agree with Claire, I don't want to ever do that again."

"What happened?" Pete asked excitedly, anxious for another good story.

Steven turned to look at Claire, wondering if he should tell them. Claire imperceptibly shook her head no.

"Trust me, Pete," Steven said, "you don't want to know. It's something even *The Ghosts of Mason Manor* would find too distasteful to publish."

"Oh," Pete said, a little crestfallen. "Well, I'll defer to your judgment."

"Are you heading straight back to Seattle after this?" Sarah asked.

"Yes," Steven said. "I've got to get back and see if we can resuscitate Daniel. There's a lot more to do, but we've got to try."

"I hope you can," Claire said. "I always liked Daniel. He's a *good* person."

Steven thought Claire had emphasized the 'good' in such a way to suggest that he, Steven, was *not* a good person. *She probably thinks I'm awful for what I did down there,* he thought. *Or maybe I'm just letting my guilt get to me and she didn't mean that at all.*

"Thanks for *your* help, Claire," Steven said. Steven emphasized the 'your' a little to make sure she remembered she had been involved in the previous night's events.

"You're welcome," Claire said, glancing up. "I hope it all works out the way you want it to."

Seems neutral enough, Steven thought. *Drop trying to analyze her and move on.*

After eating a few more forkfuls of omelet – Steven felt Sarah made a killer omelet – he set down his utensils and thanked the group.

"I have to run," he said as he stood, swallowing a last mouthful of coffee.

"Here," Sarah said, handing him a paper cup with a plastic lid. "Some for the road. Come back anytime. And give our best to Roy. And Eliza."

"Will do, thanks," Steven said, giving everyone a quick wave and heading back up to his room. He quickly packed and opened the door to leave. There was Pete, standing in the hallway, waiting. He extended his hand towards Steven's suitcase.

"Really?" Steven said.

"I told you you'd never carry your bags in this establishment," Pete said smiling, "and I meant it."

◊

Eight hours later Steven pulled his car into his driveway and toted his suitcase into his house. Eliza and Roy were inside, pouring over the book.

"Hello," he said to them. Neither turned to look.

"Oh, hi," Eliza said, continuing to stare down at the pages.

"How'd it go?" Roy asked, scanning the page with Eliza.

"Looks like you've decided to share the book with her," Steven said to Roy. "Did she offer you money?"

"Kind of," Roy said. "We're trying to understand these other two objects Daniel received from Sam. So far we've not uncovered much, but you know this book, there's always something to distract your attention. She's got me explaining petrahids."

"What are petrahids?" Steven asked.

"Never mind that now," Eliza said, "how'd it go with Claire at the manor?"

"Success," Steven said, brandishing the matter knife. He handed it to Roy.

"Good, it's full," Roy said.

"It was one of the worst experiences of my life," Steven said. "I can see why it's contraband and I can see why Jurgen was selling it to people; I expect people will pay to buy some rather than have to collect it in person. It was unpleasant in the extreme."

"Well, I'm glad you at least had success," Roy said. "Sam is a no-go. He only wants to get younger."

"That's OK," Steven said, "I may have a solution."

"What?" Roy asked.

"Garth," Steven replied. "He called me for a status update while I was driving back. I explained to him what's going on and he thinks he can help. He wants to meet with us as soon as we can get down to Olympia. I told him we'd try to make it down tonight."

Steven looked at Eliza.

"Go," she said. "I'll stay here with Daniel. He's doing OK. And I can finish up the recipes."

"All right," Steven said. "Do you mind driving, Dad? I'm tired."

"Well it's not an American car," Roy said, "but I suppose I can drive it since this is urgent."

Steven knew Roy was poking at him, but he resisted the urge to take Roy's bait and get into an argument about foreign cars. He just didn't have the energy, and he wanted to save what he had for the meeting with Garth.

"We'll be back," Steven said to Eliza, "in four or five hours, depending on traffic. Let's go, dad."

"Just a second," Roy said, walking into another room. He returned carrying a large box by a handle. The box was covered with a cloth.

"What's that?" Steven asked.

Roy raised the cloth and Steven saw that the box was actually a cage. Inside the cage was a rat.

"Where'd you get it?" Steven asked.

"Petco," Roy said. "The cage too. Cheap."

"Why? Why do you have a rat?" Steven said.

"If Garth can help us, we may need it," Roy said. "I bought it on my way up to meet with Sam."

"Why would we need a rat?"

"If Sam had agreed to the fusing, we'd have needed a way to physically bring him here, to Daniel."

"You're telling me Sam would have gone into the rat?" Steven said.

"It's called possession," Roy said. "And yes, that's exactly what would have happened. If Garth has found a soul willing to fuse with Daniel, we'll need this rat to bring it back."

"You've done this before?" Steven asked.

"Possession?" Roy said. "No, never. Just read about it."

"Great," Steven said, a little sarcastically. "Just make sure that rat doesn't get out of that cage."

◊

Steven told Roy all about his adventure in the basement of Mason Manor with Claire as they drove to Olympia.

"Claire sounds a little too goody two shoes for my tastes," Roy said.

"No," Steven said, shaking his head. "No, she's not, I'm making it sound worse than it was."

"She seemed a little smug when we met her in Oregon before," Roy said. "And that Volkswagen. I'll bet she's one of those peace and love people. They always think they're better than everyone else."

"No, you've taken this the wrong way. It wasn't like that."

"Quit defending her."

Steven knew he wouldn't win this argument either. Roy was always crass and abrasive. It was a miracle Eliza had tolerated him being stuck with him overnight. Then again, Eliza seemed to get along with everybody, and he knew Roy liked her. Maybe he went easy on her.

"Gotta hand it to you, collecting that matter with the knife sounds rough," Roy said. "I'm proud of you for seeing it through."

"I'm not proud of myself," Steven said. "I felt horrible. I tricked the guy, then I took it from him while he was being eaten."

"I'll bet hippie Claire standing there giving you shit for it didn't help," Roy said.

"She didn't give me shit for it," Steven said. "She didn't have to. It was awful regardless."

"Everything in this world either eats or gets eaten," Roy said. "Sounds to me like the creature was right. That boy can finally have some peace instead of slitting his throat all night long. So it's not as bad as all that."

"You didn't have to drag that blade along his legs," Steven said. "It felt wrong in every way. Like I was stealing something from him by slicing it off him. Imagine if I came up to you and cut off part of you."

"The way you told it," Roy said, "he was a minute away from being swallowed whole. So what's the difference?"

Steven thought about this. He kept thinking of ghosts as people, but they weren't, not really. The rules that applied to humans didn't apply to ghosts. And the only reason humans weren't devoured by other creatures was because they'd reached the top of the food chain. Apparently ghosts hadn't. *Maybe that's just the way it is,* he thought.

"Pete and Sarah doing OK?" Roy asked, changing the subject.

"Yes," Steven said, "they passed along their best wishes to you. The hotel was full. It was strange to see the dining hall full of people for breakfast."

"Yes, that would seem odd," Roy said. "I got so used to it being empty."

They chatted more about the manor; it made the drive to Olympia go quickly. Soon they were pulling up at Tall Pines.

They got out of the car and walked to the main building. It was night, and there were lights illuminating the landscape. It looked nice.

"You ever put me in one of these things," Roy said, "I'll disinherit you."

"It's actually quite nice inside," Steven said. "I was surprised."

"Yes, that's how it starts," Roy said. "Mark my word: dis-in-her-it," he said, emphasizing each syllable.

"As long as you're well behaved," Steven said, "I can't see any reason to lock you up in one of these. But step out of line..."

"Bah," Roy said. "You'd be back every day wanting help with this, that, or the other," he said, opening the front doors and stepping inside.

Steven could see the change in Roy's face as he saw the plushness of the lobby. Roy was surprised, but he wasn't going to let Steven know. He wiped a scowl back over his face.

"What a dump," Roy said, glancing around.

They made their way to the receptionist, telling her they were here to visit Garth. The receptionist called up to Garth's apartment and spoke with him briefly.

"Mr. Wilmon is on the third floor," the receptionist said. "Take the elevators behind me to the third floor, and turn right when you exit. He's in number thirty-seven. Please use the bell to ring the door, don't knock."

"Why can't we knock?" Roy asked indignantly.

"Because many of our guests are hard of hearing, while others are not. We've fine-tuned the bell for each guest to be loud enough within their apartment so they can hear it, but not so loud that it will disturb other neighbors, which loud knocking might do."

"Well, that's very well planned out," Steven said. "Sounds like you've really tailored things here for the needs of older people, to make it comfortable for them."

"That's enough," Roy said, pulling Steven away from the reception desk. "Come on."

They walked to the elevator and took it to Garth's floor. When they found his apartment, the door was ajar. Steven opened it and walked in.

"Garth?"

"Come in," Garth said from inside. Steven and Roy walked down a short hallway and into a large living room that was immaculately decorated. Floor to ceiling windows overlooked the bay. The furniture looked expensive and the artwork on the walls made Steven feel he needed to be careful what he touched. Garth was behind a bar on the other side of the room.

"Come in, sit down!" Garth said, waving to the sofas in the middle of the room. "I was just making myself a drink. What can I make for you?"

"Gin and tonic," Roy said without hesitation. He walked over to a nearby leather chair and sat.

"You must be Roy," Garth said. "Steven told me about you."

"Good things I hope," Roy said.

"The best," Garth replied. "And Steven, what can I make you?"

Steven really didn't feel like drinking, but he didn't want to seem impolite, and since he hoped Garth was going to offer them some help, he felt he'd better stay on Garth's better side.

"A vodka and water, on the rocks," he said.

"Coming right up," Garth said, his hands busy behind the counter of the bar. They heard the clink of ice as Garth mixed.

"This is impressive," Steven said. "Very nice place, Garth."

"Thank you," he said. "You can tell I was lying to you earlier when I told you I didn't have money."

"Apparently," Steven said. Garth came around the bar with a glass in each hand, giving one to Steven and the other to Roy, who thanked him. He returned to the bar to retrieve his own, then approached them for a toast.

"Here's to what I hope will be a successful plan," he said, raising his glass. Steven and Roy joined him and they all drank.

"You said you thought you might have a solution?" said.

"Yes," Garth said. "Sean."

"Sean?" Steven said. "Your brother?"

"Yes," Garth said. "He died many years ago, when he was forty. About Daniel's age."

"He'd have to be a ghost," Roy said, "or it will be extremely hard to rouse him."

"Oh, he's a ghost," Garth said. "I talk with him all the time."

Steven looked at Roy. He didn't know if Garth really did talk with Sean, or if some dementia was showing. Garth had seemed lucent and coherent when they had talked with him days ago. Old age plays funny tricks on people.

"How do you talk to him?" Roy asked.

"I close my eyes," Garth said, "and I think about him. Eventually he comes, and we talk. He's always been very protective of me. That seems to have carried over after his death."

"How often do you talk to him?" Steven asked.

"We used to speak two or three time a week, before he passed," Garth said. "That didn't stop after he died. We kept talking."

"When was the last time you talked?" Roy asked.

"Last night," Garth said. "I told him all about your visit, Steven. He was very concerned. He felt very badly that Frank was escaping the cage. I haven't yet told him the latest."

"You think Sean will be interested in helping Daniel?" Steven asked.

"I think so," Garth said. "I think he'd jump at the chance to be able to physically move again. He's mentioned it many times. I think his desire for that is one of the reasons he hasn't moved on. And me, of course."

"Yes," said Steven. "Do you think he realizes he'd be sharing a body with someone else?"

"I don't know, we'll have to talk to him about that," Garth said. "I was thinking, if you two are agreeable to it, that we should try contacting him now and ascertain his interest. If he's willing, you've got your solution to bring Daniel back."

"Would you mind if I go into a trance while you speak with him?" Roy asked. "And Steven as well? We should be able to join you in your conversation with him, provided he's willing to speak to us."

"Yes, please do," Garth said. "Is there anything you need from me?"

"No," Roy said. "I'll put on this blindfold. If you'll proceed to contact Sean, I'll be able to witness it. When Sean appears, I'll signal Steven, and he'll join my trance."

"Good, that sounds fine," Garth said, rising to dim the lights. He returned to his chair and sat down. "Everyone ready?"

Steven tied the blindfold around Roy's head. "Ready here," he said, standing behind Roy. Garth closed his eyes.

Steven turned to look out the windows. The dim light from the bay illuminated the three men inside the apartment and Steven's eyes adjusted to it quickly. He could see lights on the bay; boats, restaurants along the shore, the taillights of cars on Highway 101 in the distance. He stared out at the beautiful sight for several minutes, expecting it to take a while before contact was made. He was startled when Roy spoke.

"Steven?"

"Yes, I'm here," Steven answered.

"Would you go down to the car and get the cage?" Roy said.

"Shouldn't we speak to Sean first?" he asked.

"We already have," Roy answered. "He's agreed to help."

"Wow," Steven said, "that was fast. Usually takes longer."

"Not this time," Roy said. "Sean's been with us since we walked into the apartment. He's ready to go. Can you get the cage please?"

"On my way," Steven said.

He slipped out the door, leaving it ajar so he could get back in without disturbing the two men. He went down to the car and retrieved the cage. The receptionist smiled at him as he returned, but eyed the covered cage he brought back with him. Steven made his way to the elevator quickly and back into Garth's apartment. He set the cage on a coffee table between Roy and Garth, and removed the cloth.

"The cage is here," Steven said.

There was silence for another minute. The rat was sitting quietly, but suddenly became very active, squealing and banging against the wire sides of the cage. Then as suddenly as it had started, the rat calmed, and sat quietly again in the cage. Roy removed his blindfold.

"Can you get the lights, Steven?" Garth asked. "They're against the wall there."

The switch was within arm's length of where Steven was standing. He flipped the switch and the lights in the room slowly rose to their previous levels.

"That went smoother than I expected," Roy said.

"The rat didn't seem too happy about it," Steven said, walking towards the cage.

Garth rose from his seat and approached the cage as well. He stared into it, looking at the rat.

"So Sean is in there?" Garth asked.

"I believe so," Roy said. "Steven, would you call Eliza? Tell her to have everything ready when we get back. We'll want to do this quickly."

"Would you mind if I come with you?" Garth said. "I'd very much like to see this. I can hire a car to bring me back after."

Steven and Roy looked at each other. "I don't see why not," Steven said. "Get your things and we'll go."

Twelve

When they arrived at Steven's, Eliza had Daniel ready to go. He was laid out on the guest bed, naked, with a towel draped over his waist. A thin, clear, mucus-like substance was waiting in a large salad bowl on the nightstand, along with a Mason jar filled with a clear liquid. Roy brought the cage into the room and sat it at the foot of the bed, next to Daniel's leg.

"It worked?" Eliza asked.

"Yes, Sean is here," Roy said, motioning to the rat.

Steven introduced Garth to Eliza and they shook hands.

"What your brother is doing is a very kind thing," Eliza said. "You're kind to help, as well."

Garth smiled at her. Her charm was immediately disarming, and Steven could tell she'd won another convert. *Everybody likes Eliza*, Steven remembered Daniel saying.

"Let's do this," Steven said.

"All right," Roy said. "First, the salve. It's ready, Eliza?"

She reached to the nightstand, retrieving the salad bowl. "Here," she said, extending the bowl to the three gentlemen. None of them reached to take it from her. She looked back at them.

"Oh, never mind, I'll do it," she said, approaching Daniel. She dipped her hand into the substance and began to spread it over his body. She took care to make sure it covered all of him, including his hair and under the towel. She had Steven help her lift Daniel so she could coat his backside as well. Steven was grateful the substance had no smell. As Eliza applied it, he thought of the young man, so distraught over losing his son, and how he'd scraped the matter from his legs. That matter was now coating Daniel. He pushed the thought from his mind and returned to the task at hand.

"I think that's it," Eliza said, wiping her hands with a towel. "He's pretty much covered."

"The next step," said Roy, "is for Sean to fuse with Daniel. This will bring Daniel back to the present. I do not know how long he'll stay, however. The parasites might begin affecting Sean as quickly as they affected Daniel, so be ready to inject the protection quickly, Eliza."

Eliza produced a large syringe that she dipped into the Mason jar and slowly filled. Then she positioned herself near Daniel's head. She unplugged a cap that was on the end of a small tube taped to Daniel's cheek. She inserted the head of the syringe into the tube. "I'm ready," she said. "Once I inject it, it'll be in his stomach within a few seconds."

"OK," Roy said, and removed his blindfold. "Steven, if you would." He handed the blindfold to Steven, who stepped behind him and wrapped it around Roy's head.

All eyes were on Roy. He remained in the trance for several minutes before the rat began to act up again, screeching and running around the cage in a panic. It climbed the walls of the cage and stuck its nose through the bars, desperate to get out. Steven saw it push with such force that its eyes began to bulge, and he was afraid they might pop, or the thin bars of the cage give way. It continued to press, but then Steven saw the hind legs go limp, and the body of the rat slumped, lowering to the bottom of the cage. The rat's nose remained wedged in between the bars.

As the rat stilled, Daniel began to move. Steven saw his fingers extend and his elbows shift.

"Now, Eliza!" Roy said. Eliza turned her attention from Roy and focused on the syringe. She pressed the plunger and watched as the liquid ran out and into the tube, disappearing down Daniel's mouth.

For several seconds they watched as Daniel continued to move. He wasn't jerking; it was small, deliberate moves as though he was testing out his muscles. His toes curled. His neck shifted his head slightly. He continued these small movements for a couple of minutes, and then he was still.

After that, nothing. Steven feared that the procedure might have failed.

"Eliza, move back," Roy said. "They're emerging."

Steven and Eliza slipped into the flow and observed. They saw four different white centipedes chew their way out of Daniel's lower stomach. As each emerged and reached the surface they began to turn translucent. They didn't make it more than an inch or two from the hole they'd emerged from before they slowed and died.

Eliza left the flow and checked on Daniel. His breathing and pulse seemed normal. Steven and Roy remained in the flow, watching the centipedes until they had completely faded from view. Once it appeared they were gone, they exited the flow. Roy removed his blindfold.

"What happened?" Garth asked, standing in the back of the room, observing. "The rat is dead."

"Yes," Roy said, "and the fusing is complete. The parasites were driven out. As far as I can tell, we did everything according to plan."

"How is he?" Steven asked Eliza.

"Same as before," she said. "Body is perfectly fine. Whether he's made it to the present or not we won't know until he revives. How long does this salve need to stay on, Roy? The parasites are out."

"I think you can wipe it off and clean him up," Roy said.

"So now we wait," Steven said.

"Yes," Roy said, "that's all we can do for now."

◊

It was late, and everyone decided to turn in for the night. Garth asked if he could stay, and Roy offered to put him up for the night at his place. Steven offered to sleep on the couch and give Eliza his bed, but Eliza said she'd sit up with Daniel for a while to keep an eye on him.

When Steven woke the next morning, he found Eliza sitting with Daniel in the living room. Steven walked up to Daniel and gave him a big hug. "Welcome back," he said, squeezing him. "We thought we'd lost you."

"I thought I was lost," Daniel said. "Literally."

"Looks like you found the coffee," Steven said, returning to the kitchen to pour himself some.

"Tastes so good," Daniel said, staring at his mug.

"How is he, physically?" Steven asked Eliza.

"Seems fine," Eliza said. "All of his vitals are normal."

"I don't feel fine," Daniel said. "I feel…different."

"Eliza told you what we had to do?" Steven asked.

"Yes," Daniel said, "and he's here. I can access all of his memories. He hasn't tried to take control, but I'm afraid to just turn things over to him and let him do that."

"Garth offered Sean as a solution," Steven said. "He's staying at Roy's. I'll call them and let them know you're OK. I expect they'll want to come over and see you."

"Sure," Daniel said. "I guess Sean saved me, in a way. So I guess I'm grateful he's here. But it's strange, you know, having someone else inside you, knowing they're there."

"I'll bet," Steven said, trying to imagine it.

"Can't tell you how good this coffee is," Daniel said, taking another long sip.

"He's been drinking it all morning," Eliza said. "This is the second pot."

Steven rose to call Roy and Garth, and while waiting for them to arrive he took a quick shower and got cleaned up. As he dressed he could hear Roy and Garth arriving, chatting with Eliza and Daniel. He joined them in the living room.

"Thank you, Garth," Daniel said. "It's really quite extraordinary."

"You're welcome," Garth said. "But it was actually Sean's idea. I told him what had happened, and he offered. He wanted to do it."

"Why do you suppose that is?" Eliza asked.

"Sean died young," Garth replied. "He was about your age when he passed. I don't think he felt he'd done all he wanted to in life. He became a ghost almost immediately; he started visiting me the week after he died and has visited ever since. Part of it was his natural inclination to protect me, which he'd been doing his whole life. But part of it was regret, I think. Missed opportunities. I'm hoping that he's able to enjoy life for a few more years with you, Daniel. I'll pass on soon, so that'll remove that excuse. Whenever your day comes, Daniel, I'm hoping he'll feel OK with just moving on."

"He wants to talk to you," Daniel said. "I can feel him. But to let him, I'd have to give up control. I'm scared to do that. I don't know if I'd get it back. It's like agreeing to let a stranger drive your car, but in this case it's your life – how do I know he'll return it?"

"I know Sean," Garth said. "You have nothing to fear. He will give it back."

"I've begun to let it happen a couple of times this morning," Daniel said, "because he's anxious. I can tell he really wants control. But the feeling as you let it happen – it's like what I imagine dying to be."

"Like what we saw with the rat in the cage," Roy said. "The fear of dying, of losing yourself. Very frightening."

"You take it in your own time," Garth said. "Sean will understand."

"What was it like before you came back?" Steven asked.

"Hard to describe," Daniel replied. "I guess I'd call it like being in a huge house of mirrors. All the options looked the same, like reflections of myself. I'd choose a path, walk down it, and find myself somewhere. No idea where. No idea what year or time it was, no idea what place. I could observe what was going on there, but I couldn't interact – I had no body. I could back out of it and be in the house of mirrors again. That's why I felt lost. I knew I'd never find you all. But it was absolutely fascinating from an academic perspective."

"For someone like you, all obsessed with time," Eliza said, smiling, "that might have been heaven for you. Maybe we should have left you there. For a while longer, at least."

"Wouldn't have mattered," Daniel said. "I felt like I was there for an instant and for an eternity. Time completely lost meaning in the house of mirrors. Once I went into a moment I felt time return, as I saw people and things moving through time. But when I pulled back time disappeared. So I felt like I was there forever, from the first moment I was there. Kinda hard to explain."

"Kinda hard for our linear-thinking brains to comprehend," Steven said. "But I think I get the drift."

"Well, the main thing is that you're healthy and you've survived it," Garth said. "I think I'll go back to Olympia. You take your time with Sean. I'll leave you my number so you can reach me if you want to."

"I'm sure Sean will emerge at some point," Daniel said. "Thanks for being patient."

Garth said his goodbyes to everyone while waiting for the car to pick him up. Soon he was out the door and on his way back home. Eliza made another pot of coffee. Between Roy and Garth's arrival and Daniel's craving for it, the coffee maker was getting a lot of use. Roy said he'd go out and pick up some donuts, and Steven went into another room to call Jason.

When Eliza returned to the living room, Daniel was looking at the objects Sam had given to him when he gave him the parasites. "I know what these are now," he said.

"Because of your experience?" she asked.

"Yes," Daniel replied. "Because of that. This one is a chronosphere, as I suspected" he said, lifting up one of the objects. "And that one," he said, pointing to one on the coffee table in front of him, "holds a minor demon."

"A minor demon?" Eliza asked.

"It's a time demon," Daniel said. "You know, I'll bet this means I can figure out what each of the items in my collection does." He lit up, excited. "I've got to get back to Spokane!"

"Slow down," Eliza said. "How about we rest up for the day here. I'd like to make sure you're OK first. Then, if you don't mind, I'll drive you back in your car, and I'll fly home from Spokane."

"You don't have to do that," Daniel said. "I'm fine."

Eliza cocked her head to the side and stared at him. It was a look Daniel was familiar with.

"Then again," he said, "I sure would enjoy the company on the drive back." He smiled at her.

"Great, it's settled. We'll leave tomorrow morning. The rest of today I want you to take it easy. Your body is adjusting after several days on a feeding tube and IV."

Daniel nodded his head in agreement, then stood up and walked into the kitchen. "Do we have any orange juice? Or maybe some water…"

◊

Steven's call to Jason went well. The nightmares had ended and he was feeling better. Steven was relieved. But Jason wanted to come over and see him, saying he had something important he wanted to talk to him about. Steven felt dread in the pit of his stomach, but masked it and told Jason he could come over anytime. Jason said he'd be there in an hour. *Damn, I made him that promise,* Steven thought. *I'll bet he's coming over to cash it in.*

Steven rejoined Eliza and Daniel in the living room. He wanted to keep an eye on Daniel to make sure he was all right, but with Eliza there he didn't feel too concerned. And he was enjoying the stories Daniel was telling about the different moments he'd accessed and observed. Daniel was energized and excited by the events. He could also tell that Daniel was worried about Sean.

At one point Daniel stopped talking, as though he had lost his train of thought and was trying to remember something. As he paused, Eliza and Steven looked at each other, concerned. Then he resumed talking, on an entirely different subject. Steven wrote it off to the confusion he must feel, having Sean inside him and having gone through what he had in the past 24 hours.

Roy returned with the donuts and joined in on the conversation. Daniel asked Roy how the possession events had occurred, and Roy was describing the process when Jason arrived. Steven introduced everyone to Jason.

"Well, aren't you a handsome young man," Eliza said, shaking his hand. "The apple didn't fall far from the tree."

Steven could feel his cheeks flushing a little. Jason didn't seem fazed by the comment.

"Dad, could I talk to you?" Jason asked, once the introductions were done and people had returned to their conversations. "Privately?"

"Sure," Steven said. "Let's go in here." He led Jason to the back bedroom.

Once they were both inside, Steven shut the door. "What did you want to talk about?" he asked.

"It's about this," Jason said, holding the rectangular object. "A friend of mine saw it. She wigged out."

"I told you to keep it to yourself," Steven said.

"And I did," Jason said, "but she came across it."

"What, you left it out?"

"No, it was on me, as we discussed."

"Then how did she…" The light bulb turned on for Steven. "Oh. I see."

"So she wigs out," Steven said. "Because she thought she knew what it was."

Steven didn't like where this was going. He wanted to be able to talk to Jason about the gift on his own terms, when he felt they were both ready. This felt like an outing, like he was being forced to either lie to his son or come clean about everything, and he wasn't ready to do that.

"What did she say about it?" Steven asked, stalling for time to think.

Before Jason could respond, they heard Eliza calling from the hallway outside the door.

"Steven! Come quickly!"

Steven looked at Jason and gave him a "hold that thought" hand gesture, then he went to the door to open it and see what Eliza wanted. She wasn't in the hallway, so he went to the living room. It was empty, but the front door to the house was wide open. He went out the door, Jason following him.

"Eliza?" he called, walking down the front deck and onto the sidewalk. Eliza was chasing after Daniel and Roy, who were further down the block. He ran after them. Jason was not far behind.

When he reached the three of them, he could tell something was wrong. Daniel was walking slowly and deliberately, his eyes fixed forward. Roy and Eliza were on either side of him, talking to him.

"What's wrong?" Steven asked.

"No idea," Roy said. "He got up and walked out the door."

"Daniel," Eliza said, "what's going on? Where are you going?"

"I have no idea," Daniel said. "I can't stop my legs. I don't have control of them."

Daniel kept walking. They were approaching an intersection, and Daniel wasn't slowing, not caring about traffic. They surrounded him, trying to stop him.

"Daniel, you're walking into traffic," Steven said. "We're going to stop you."

"Please do," he said. Steven reached out to grab him, but Daniel brushed off his hold.

"I didn't do that," Daniel said, continuing to walk and now halfway through the intersection. They held their hands up to stop the cars that were coming. The cars slowed and let them pass.

"Dad, what's wrong with him?" Jason asked.

"Not now, Jason," Steven said.

"Do you think it's Sean?" Eliza asked. "Is it Sean controlling you, Daniel?"

"I don't know," Daniel said. "Maybe. I can't say. It's the damndest thing. I'm so incredibly thirsty."

"If it was Sean," Roy said, "I don't think Daniel's personality would be at the forefront like this."

"Maybe it's Sean trying to gain control," Steven offered, "and only succeeding half way."

"Why would Sean make him get up and walk?" Eliza said.

"Maybe Sean is trying to figure out how to control him?" Steven said.

"What are you guys talking about?" Jason asked.

"Jason, please, not now," Steven said.

Daniel was crossing into the grassy area that sloped down to Lake Washington. He walked over a jogger's trail and continued down the slope. In another minute he'd be at the lake's edge.

"If he tries to go into the water," Steven said, "I say we all grab him and physically restrain him."

"Agreed," Eliza said.

They continued to surround him. Steven stood in front of him, facing him, but Daniel was not deterred and kept walking. Daniel looked at Steven. "I can't stop it," he said. As they got closer to the water, Daniel began to look scared.

"Are you going to go into the water?" Steven asked, walking backwards. He was now a couple of yards from the water's edge. He extended his arm and placed his hand on Daniel's chest, pressing him back. Daniel met the resistance and pressed forward.

"I don't know," he said. Tears were beginning to form around the edges of his eyes. "I don't know. Help me, please."

When Daniel was about five feet from the water, he stopped. They all took a step back from him.

Daniel slowly bent down and then fell forward, on his hands and knees. He moved a few more feet towards the water.

"Get ready to grab him," Steven said.

Daniel stopped as his hands came within a foot of the water's edge. His head started to shake.

"What the fuck?" Jason said.

"The River," Roy said. "Quickly."

Eliza and Steven both jumped into the flow. Roy was already there.

Steven saw the back of Daniel's head split apart, and a translucent stalk about two inches in diameter began to grow out of it, rapidly. He could hear Daniel crying, gasping for air.

What is happening to him? Eliza thought.

I have no idea, Steven thought.

As they watched, the stalk extended upward about two feet. A joint formed, and the stalk bent, growing rapidly towards the water. Within seconds it extended another four or five feet out from the joint. A bulb formed on the end of the stalk and grew, like a balloon filling with air. It popped, and dozens of smaller bulbs fell lightly out of it. They drifted down to the water, some moved by the air to spots several feet away. When they hit the water, Steven saw small fins emerge and they descended below the surface. Within a few more seconds they had all disappeared below the water.

They exited the flow. Daniel was still on his hands and knees at the water's edge. Eliza knelt down to feel his neck. There was no pulse.

"Call an ambulance," Steven said to Jason, knowing he'd have his cell phone on him. "Do it now."

Daniel remained frozen. Steven bent down to look at him. He was rigid and unmoving. His mouth was stretched open as though he'd been trying to scream, and his eyes were bulging out of his head. Steven turned away, holding his hand over his mouth.

People walking the jogger's trail had begun to stop. A couple had come over.

"Is he all right?" a man asked, his wife with him.

"We've called 911," Roy said. "We think he might have had a seizure."

After a couple of minutes passed they could hear the siren in the distance. The medical crew turned him over onto his back and lowered his arms and legs. They worked with him for a few moments, but he didn't recover. One of the medics told Eliza that he was dead.

Things were going by in a blur. Steven was only catching pieces of what was happening, here and there. He watched as they carried the body bag on a stretcher back to the ambulance and placed him inside. Eliza was crying and Roy was holding her. Jason stood next to Steven, unsure if he should say anything.

"What just happened, Dad?" Jason asked.

"Honestly, son, I don't know. I really don't."

"He had a seizure?"

"That's what they think."

"But you don't think that, do you?"

"Why would you ask me that?"

"When he reached the water, all three of you knew something else was going on. I saw it on your faces. Right after Grandpa Roy said 'the River.'"

Steven realized the time had come, whether he wanted it to or not. It was here. He was going to have to tell Jason about the gift, and about him and Roy. It couldn't be a worse time, with Daniel gone, Eliza upset, and Garth – they would have to let Garth know that Sean was probably gone now too. He wanted to get back to the house and find out from Roy and Eliza what their perspectives were on what they had just seen, but he couldn't do that with Jason here, not until after he had a chance to introduce Jason to this world properly.

Fuck it, he thought. *Why fight it?*

"You're about to jump right into the deep end of the pool," Steven told him. "You sure you're ready for that?"

"I'd rather know than not," Jason said.

"Come on then," Steven said. "Let's go back to the house."

He led Jason, Roy, and a sobbing Eliza back up the embankment, past the onlookers, and up the street towards his home.

Thirteen

They walked back to Steven's house and fell into the chairs and sofas in the living room. They sat quietly for a while, Eliza stifling an occasional sob.

"I'd like to know what's happening," Jason said. "I know there's a lot you're not telling me."

Steven sighed. "I always planned on telling you," he said, "but not like this. Still, here we are, so here goes. Your father and my father can enter a place called 'the River' when we want to. It's a flow all around us that most people can't see or access. You see things differently from within it.

"What happened to Daniel," Steven continued, "that we could see, that you couldn't, was a long stalk emerging from his head. It extended over the water, and some kind of seeds emerged from it, falling into the water and then disappearing below the surface."

Jason's mouth hung open.

"I'm guessing that wasn't what you were expecting to hear," Steven said.

"So this is how you're going to dump it on him?" Roy said. "Like this?"

"Wasn't how I'd planned it," Steven said, "but yes, like this. He wanted to know."

"Just because he wanted to know doesn't mean you have to tell him."

"Frankly, Dad, I'm sick of secrets and I'm sick of half-assed work. This is partly your fault."

"My fault? How do you figure that?"

"It was your father who fucked this up. He should have eliminated Frank, not caged him. He didn't solve a problem, he created one."

"Frank was abusing those boys," Roy said defiantly. "He did what he thought was the right thing to do."

"It wasn't the right thing, that's my point," Steven said. "He should have stayed out of it if he couldn't actually solve it."

"If he'd stayed out of it, Sean and Garth might not have survived. Frank might have killed them."

"And Daniel might be alive, now."

"You want to say all this, in front of your boy?"

Jason's mouth hadn't yet closed. He was looking from Roy to Steven, like a tennis match.

"Why not?" Steven answered. "Why not let him see how his parents and grandparents and great-grandparents have fucked it all up? Maybe then he'll think twice before he steps in. Or maybe he'll actually finish something once he starts it, unlike you."

"What's that supposed to mean?"

"In the short time I've worked with you in this shitty business, you've left two monsters alive. Michael and Jurgen. Time bombs waiting to come back and blow up in our faces, just like Frank came back. How many more time bombs are there, Dad? How many more did you and your fathers create? Don't you think he should know about them, since he's going to have to clean up all of the shit you were too lazy to clean up?"

Roy stood up. He walked over to Jason and looked down at him. "Your father is a disrespectful bastard," he said. Then he turned and walked out the door, slamming it as he left.

"Fucking prick," Steven said as the slam reverberated through the house.

Jason was looking at the floor, unsure of what to say or think. He looked up at Steven.

Steven was fuming over Roy. He glanced over to Jason and saw him looking at him.

"Welcome to the deep end," he said.

◊

Eliza was packing up Daniel's things. She had piled all of the medical supplies into a corner of the guest room. It had been an hour since Roy had left. Steven had sent Jason home, telling him they'd talk more tomorrow. Steven stepped into the guest room to see how Eliza was doing.

"I'm so sorry," Steven said.

"It's not your fault," she said. "And it's not Roy's, either."

"I know," Steven said. "I'm just angry and frustrated. Daniel was a good friend to you. I guess the option of Troy ever knowing him is gone now."

"True," she said. She was folding clothes, placing them in Daniel's bag. "Who knows how that might have gone. You know, I'd like to get to Daniel's place and try to salvage some of his time artifacts before his family gets to them. They won't know what they are, they'll just throw them away as trash. I might be able to get them to sell me his library. It would be nice to try and preserve his collection, it's his legacy. Maybe Troy can see that someday."

"I'll come with you if you want," Steven said.

"That's kind of you to offer, but I think I'd rather do it on my own," she said. "I think you'll have your hands full here, with Roy and Jason. There's a lot you need to do on both fronts."

"I know. I probably could have handled that better. But I'm just so tired of the half-assed approach. Is this normal? Is this how you do it?"

"Well, I don't kill people, if that's what you're asking."

"Michael was a child killer. Jurgen, well you know about him. Both deserved to die."

"If the Manitou didn't finish Jurgen off, there was a reason for that. I promise you."

"What reason could there be? Jurgen was a horrible person."

"Justice, Steven. It measured out the exact amount of justice for what he'd done. You might have misjudged his history."

"And Michael? Why leave him alive?"

"That was Roy's doing?"

"Yes, and I was too inexperienced to argue with him. I didn't like the decision at the time, and I told him so. But he thought it was best to 'let sleeping dogs lie,' those were his words."

"Roy is a smart man," she said, "and he's had many years of experience, whereas you've had less than one. I don't know the whole story, but I do know Roy, and if he thought it was best to leave Michael alone, there had to be good reasons for it. Either reasons you're not telling me or that you don't know."

"Arrrrghhhh!" Steven said in frustration, raising his hands over his head and leaving the room to walk into his bedroom.

"Steven, come here," Eliza said. He stopped and returned to the guest bedroom.

"What?" he asked.

"Look at these," she said, holding the objects Daniel had been examining earlier in the day.

"He got those from Sam," Steven said. "Wasn't sure what they'd do."

"Yes, he told me. But he also figured them out, this morning. He told me what they were."

"Really?" Steven asked.

"He said this one was a chronosphere, and this one held a demon. A minor demon."

"Oh?" Steven said, approaching her to look more closely at the objects.

"He said the demon was a time demon."

"What's that?"

"I don't know, but I would like to find out. I remember a section on demons in Roy's book, when we were looking through it while you were in Oregon. I'd like to see if it has more information on this."

"I need to apologize to him," Steven said. "How about we go over there first thing in the morning?"

"Deal."

"I think I'm going to turn in. Are you going to be all right?"

"Yes," she said, "I just want to finish packing up these things of his, and I'll be turning in as well."

She turned to look at him, and he saw the pain in her eyes. He extended his arms and she gave him a long hug. She started to cry again.

"I really am sorry," Steven said. "So sorry."

◊

The next morning Steven called Roy to tell him they were coming over. Roy didn't pick up, so Steven left him a message.

"Look, I know you're pissed at me and that's why you're not answering your phone. But Eliza and I are coming over, so try to look respectable." He hung up.

"Nice," she said. "That'll start things on the right foot."

"He's much worse than me," Steven said. "You should see him sometimes."

Eliza smiled. "Let's go."

When they arrived at Roy's, they knocked but didn't get a response at the door.

"Listen, Roy, I know you're in there. Open up. Eliza's out here in the cold."

The door finally opened and a grumpy Roy turned without greeting them and walked back into the house. Steven and Eliza went inside.

"Here to berate me some more?" Roy said.

"No," Steven said. "The opposite. I'm here to apologize."

"You can shove your apology up your ass," Roy said, sitting at the kitchen table. "Eliza, would you like some coffee?"

"Thank you, Roy, that'd be nice."

He poured her a mug and handed it to her, then replaced the pot in the coffee maker.

"None for me, that's my penalty for being mean to you last night?" Steven said.

"Eliza, do you hear a buzzing sound? Like the sound of a buzzing ungrateful piss-ant?"

"I'm staying out of this," she said.

"She urged me to come over and apologize," Steven said. "And I mean to. I'm sorry, Dad, I shouldn't have said those things to you, especially in front of Jason."

"You needn't have urged him to," Roy said to Eliza. "He was bound to come over sooner or later, as soon as he needed something. I'll bet he needs something now, am I right?"

"Actually I'm the one who needs something," Eliza said, taking some of the heat away from Steven. "These objects Sam gave Daniel. Daniel knew what they were yesterday, after he woke up. One of them holds a time demon. I was hoping you'd help me look through your book for information on it." She smiled.

"I'd be delighted to help you," he said. "You're a kind person who is always respectful and grateful, unlike others. Let me get the book." He rose and walked into the back bedroom, and returned with the book, which he sat between himself and Eliza where they could both see it as he turned the pages.

Steven sighed and let Roy help Eliza without his involvement. He'd apologized, and he knew that he just needed to let it sink in with Roy, and he'd accept it. But not right at first – Roy would make him pay first.

Steven walked over to the chairs in the living room and sat in one of them.

"He often sulked as a child," Roy said to Eliza as they scanned the pages. "A very bad habit, hard to grow out of."

Steven bit his lip and stayed seated in the chair. He pulled out his phone to check his messages and kill some time while Eliza and Roy worked their way through the book.

"I know I saw a section on demons when we were looking through it the other day," Eliza said.

"That would be back in the Thomas pages," Roy said, flipping to the earlier sections of the book.

"Yes, here it is," Eliza said. "Wow, he has quite a catalog here. Dozens of them."

"Here's the info on how to release demons from objects," Roy said.

Eliza kept scanning the list, looking for something related to time.

"Found it!" she said, delighted. Steven got up out of his chair and joined them.

She read the paragraphs under the entry she'd marked with her finger. "It's simple," she said.

"What?" Steven asked. "How does it work?"

"Well," she said, turning to look at Roy and Steven, "the steps Roy found will release it from the object. The demon can traverse time and will take you where you want to go and back, but for a price."

"Let me guess," Steven said. "A soul."

"It's always souls with demons," Roy said.

"Yes," Eliza said, "which is why they're not often used. If you don't have a soul to offer up to the demon, it'll take you instead. So it's a dangerous move. But it's what I suspected."

"Well, hold onto it, and it can be part of the collection you save for Troy," Steven said.

"Oh, no," Eliza said. "I was thinking something else."

"Such as?" Roy asked.

"I was hoping you'd be willing to use it."

"Use it?" Steven asked. "How?"

"Roy," she said, "I was hoping you'd convince David to use this demon to go back to 1933 and kill Frank. Outright."

Roy was taken back, and Steven was stunned.

"Kill him, instead of cage him?" Roy asked once he had regained himself.

"Yes," she said. "With Frank dead, he can't come back to cause the trouble eighty years later."

"Oh, yes he can," Steven said. "He'll just be a ghost, but he can come back. They always can."

"Not if the demon takes his soul right after David kills him."

They both sat stunned again. Eliza saw the slightly confused look on their faces.

"You contact David," she said. "You explain to him the deal to cut with the demon, which is, if he will take him back to 1933 so he can kill Frank, the demon can have Frank's soul as payment for the trip. David can correct the mistake of caging Frank, and we'll get Daniel back, because none of this would have happened."

"But," Steven said, "if this never happened, there would have been no object for David to use to go back and correct anything. Doesn't that cause our timeline to...implode or something?"

"Exactly," she said. "Look, time has more continuity than people think. It was Daniel's belief that there are an infinite number of simultaneous timelines playing out. We're in all of them, but we're only aware of one of them because that's all our mind can handle. If this timeline ends, we'll instantly become aware of another that's at the same point in time. We won't even be aware of the shift. They're all essentially the same, with just minor differences. I'm fine with this timeline we're in imploding. I want to go to the one that has Frank dead and Daniel alive."

"How do you know so much about this?" Roy asked.

"I lived with a time freak for several years, Roy," she said. "You pick up things."

"What do you think, Dad?" Steven asked Roy.

"As much as the idea of a timeline blipping out unnerves me," Roy said, looking at them, "I'll try. I'll ask David if he'll do it."

"Thank you," Eliza said.

"Will he be hard to reach?" Steven asked. "When's the last time you talked to him?"

"No, he'll be easy to reach," Roy said. "I talk to him every morning."

◊

Although things between Roy and Steven were thawing a little, Roy didn't want Steven to sit in on his trance to contact David, saying he was still too pissed at him for it to work. Roy and Eliza conducted the trance alone, and Steven waited in the guest bedroom at Roy's, where he'd slept months back when he and Roy were fighting the ghosts that used to haunt Steven's house. The room used to be Steven and his brother Bernard's room when they were kids. He'd had too much coffee to drift off to sleep, so he busied himself with his phone, reading the news, playing mindless finger games. After a half an hour of solitude Eliza came to his door.

"We're done," she said as she opened it. It felt to Steven like he was being let out of his room after being grounded.

Probably how Roy wanted it to feel, he thought. *Well I've apologized and I've paid my penance, things better be balanced out now.*

"And?" Steven asked, walking back into the living room where Roy sat.

"I don't know what I was thinking," Roy said. "He's fine with the plan, but it doesn't matter what he thinks."

Steven looked confused.

"We realized as we were working it out with him," Eliza said, "that he can't go back with the demon because he's not physical."

"So one of us has to go back," Steven said.

"Yes," Eliza said, "and convince David in 1933 to handle things differently."

"How about I go back," Steven said, "and shoot him myself?"

"You can go back," Roy said, "but you won't be able to kill anybody. When you traverse time like this you can't actually do anything yourself. You can observe, you can communicate with others, but you can't change anything directly. We've got to talk to David and convince him to not help the boys cage Frank."

"And don't forget you have to convince him to kill Frank as well," Steven said, "or have you lost your concern for the welfare of the boys?"

Roy shot Steven a dirty look. "I'm trying to be civil here, piss-ant, it'd be nice if you'd meet me halfway."

"Stop, both of you," Eliza said. "You both love each other and need each other's help. And god knows I need you both right now. So please, for me, stop."

Steven and Roy both looked at Eliza, then looked away, embarrassed at their behavior.

"Who can convince David of what needs to be done?" Eliza said. "Who do you think he will listen to?"

"Probably me," Roy said. "I can blow his mind with a few facts from the future and then tell him what needs to happen."

"And just so we're clear," Steven said, "what needs to happen is exactly what?"

"He needs to stop the boys from caging Frank," Roy said, "and he needs to find a way to kill Frank instead."

"It's a tall order for a ten-year-old boy," Eliza said. "Do you think you can do it?"

"I'll try," Roy said. "That's the best I can do."

Fourteen

Roy found himself standing behind a bush in David Hall's backyard. David was swinging in a tire that hung from a large tree. They were 30 feet from the back of the house. Roy couldn't see any signs of movement in it. *Charles, my grandfather, lives in there,* he thought. *And my grandmother, Leone. She always kept a sharp eye out the kitchen window. I'll have to be careful.*

Beside him, in the flow, was a presence monitoring his actions. When Roy had released and invoked the demon, it asked for payment, and Roy explained his plan. The demon agreed to the plan, but said if anything went wrong, he'd take Roy as payment. Roy reluctantly agreed, and seconds later, Roy was in 1933.

Time to wing it, Roy thought. *Just call the boy over.*

"Davy," Roy said. "Come here."

David stopped swinging in the tire and turned to look at the source of the voice. "Who are you, mister?" He climbed off the swing and started walking in Roy's direction.

"I have something important I need to talk to you about," Roy said. "But it's a secret, so come over here and I'll tell you."

Roy guessed the 1933 mores hadn't yet made every young boy suspicious of older men. In that era, children did what they were told by any adult, family or not. He was also counting on Davy's gift to help him believe what he had to tell him.

David walked over to Roy. Roy stopped him when he was about three feet from the bush.

"Grandma Leone might be watching, so stop there, and turn away from the kitchen window," Roy said.

"Grandma Leone?" David said. "You mean my mama?"

"Yes," Roy said, "your mama."

"So what's the secret, mister?" David turned his back to the kitchen window, picked up a stick, and began drawing figures in the dirt.

"You know how you sometimes can see or feel things other people can't?" Roy said.

"Yeah," David said, "so?"

"Well, I can too," Roy said. "Your father can, too, right?"

"I think so," David said. "But he doesn't talk about it."

"Right. Do you suppose, if you ever have a son, you'd talk about it with him?"

"Sure," David said. "I'd tell him everything."

"You're going to grow up and get married, and have a son."

"Of course I will, that's what everybody does."

"And your son will have the same gift as you, and you will share it with him when he's your age."

David looked puzzled. "Who are you, mister? Is that the secret?"

"No, that's not the secret. The secret is extremely important, because it's going to save the life of your friends."

"My friends?"

"Sean and Garth."

"Oh, them. Yes, they're my friends."

"In about five or ten minutes, Garth is going to come over here, wanting you to follow him back to their garage. When you get there, you'll see that Sean has been beaten up by his father, Frank. You know Frank."

"I sure do." A look of worry crossed David's face.

"When you follow Garth across the street and into the garage, a boy inside the garage is going to give you things to help Sean and Garth get rid of Frank. This is the secret, Davy: you must not get rid of Frank that way. You must not. You have to get rid of him another way."

"What do you mean, get rid of him?"

"You'll understand when the boy explains it to you. But remember the secret I'm telling you, Davy. You must not get rid of Frank the way the boy tells you to."

"Why not?"

"Because if you do, horrible things will happen later. I've seen what happens. You must not do it."

"You had a vision?"

"In a way, yes. Horrible things happen to your son, your grandson, even your great-grandson if you do what the boy tells you."

"So what do I do?"

"The boy is going to tell you to give two items to Sean and Garth, along with some instructions. I want you to pocket the items, then take Sean and Garth out of the garage where the boy can't hear you, and tell them instead to bring Frank into the garage. When Frank comes into the garage, you need to kill him."

"Kill him? I'm no killer, mister."

"I know, but you must. If Frank stays alive, Sean and Garth will die, he'll beat them to death. Can you imagine that?"

David shook his head no.

"Will you do it?"

"I don't know. Won't I go to jail?"

"Not if it was self-defense, which you'll claim. Sean and Garth will back you up."

"How would I kill him?"

"You know where your father keeps his guns, don't you?"

"Yes, they're easy to find."

"You'll take his pistol and use that."

David was thinking, his brow furrowing. "Who's that with you?"

He definitely has the gift, Roy thought. *Sensing the demon without entering the flow.*

"He made it possible for me to have the vision and to tell you about it, before it was too late. Without him I wouldn't have been able to warn you, to save Sean and Garth."

"I don't know mister, Frank's a bad man and all that, but killing him, I don't know."

"You want to be a father, don't you, son?"

"Sure I do. Someday."

"Then think of your children. Your sons. Do you know why they're in danger?"

"No."

"Because if you help Sean and Garth use the objects the boy gives you, Frank's soul will be trapped for several years. But he knows you helped them do it. And Frank gets out of the trap, eventually. When he does, he comes after your kids. He's so angry you trapped him, he wants to kill your kids for revenge. You're either about to create a big problem, or solve a problem. But you have to choose."

"Davy! Davy!" Roy could hear Garth's yells as he approached from across the street.

"He's coming now. Remember what I've told you. The lives of your children depend upon it."

David turned to face the approaching Garth. Roy retreated back behind the bush so Garth wouldn't see him.

"Davy!" Garth yelled from across the yard. He was running full speed and he slowed only as he neared Davy, kicking up dust as he slid to a stop.

"You've got to come over. The boy in the garage, he's asking for you. Frank's beat Sean real bad. The boy wants to help. He said, 'get Davy!" Come on!" Garth turned and began running back.

David glanced over to Roy. Roy winked at him. Then David followed Garth.

◊

After half an hour David returned. He walked to the backyard, looking for Roy.

Roy was still behind the bush, waiting. "You're back."

"Yes," David said. "I did it. Well, most of it."

"What do you mean?"

"Well, they saw the boy give me something, so I had to at least give them something or they would have known something was up."

"Did you give them the objects?"

"I gave them my pocket knife," David said, "and told them to put it under Frank's bed. But I kept the box and the powder." He pulled the small wooden matchbox and paper envelope from his back pocket, showing them to Roy.

"Good boy," Roy said, feeling a huge sense of relief. At least half of the plan had worked.

"I want that pocket knife back," David said. "My grandpa gave it to me."

That would be Thomas, Roy thought. *The first writer in the book.*

"Did you tell them to bring Frank back out to the garage?" Roy asked.

"Yes," David said. "They're going to hide the pocket knife tonight. Then they're gonna get him real teed off and trick him out to the garage tomorrow."

"Tomorrow?" Roy said. "Why not now?"

"Well, if I'm gonna shoot him, which I'm not saying I am, but if I am, I need to get the gun first, don't I?"

"You could get it now."

"No way, mister. My pop should be home any minute now. I won't be able to get his gun until he goes to work tomorrow, when mama's outside hanging laundry. Any other time and I'll get caught."

Roy was concerned the demon might not go for this. Still, he had to play it out, he couldn't quit halfway. The demon would take either Frank's soul or his, and he didn't want it to be his.

"All right, tomorrow then," Roy said. "What time tomorrow?"

"I don't know for sure. We're gonna talk tomorrow after they're back from working. Then they'll get Frank all riled up and make him follow them out to the garage."

"And when he gets to the garage, you'll shoot him?"

"I suppose so. I guess so. I don't know. Are you sure he'd kill Sean and Garth if we don't kill him first?"

"I'm sure. I've seen it."

"What else have you seen?"

Roy got the impression it was a test. He sighed. "You have a son," he said. "You're smarter than your father; you lock your guns away. But your son goes looking for the guns, just like you did. He doesn't find them, but he finds a book instead. A book that your father is going to give to you one day. When your son finds that book, you're going to be proud of him, and you're going to start training him, showing him how to use his gift, the same gift you have. And you're going to write in the book, so your son knows how to use his gift, and his son is going to read it too. And they're going to remember you, and how kind you were, because you trained them, you gave them the book, and you did this thing, killing Frank. And you're going to live a long, full life, full of happiness and success. You're going to help a lot of people, friends who need help. And when you die, your son is going to be very proud of you. Very proud."

David twisted and turned as Roy spoke. Roy couldn't tell if he believed what he was telling him or not.

"OK," David said. "I'll steal pop's gun tomorrow."

"Good boy," Roy said, wanting to reach out and ruffle his hair. "You'll save Sean and Garth, remember that."

"Davy!" came Leone's voice from the house. "Dinner!"

"I gotta go," David said.

"I'll be watching tomorrow," Roy said.

"All right," David said, turning to go. "Bye."

◊

Jason arrived at Bent's five minutes later than his father. Steven had commandeered a booth, and Jason joined him, slipping into the vinyl seat.

"I figured I could lure you with a free burger," Steven said.

"I'll stay even longer if you throw in a free beer," Jason said, grabbing the menu from the edge of the table.

"How old are you? Twenty?" Steven asked. "It's called 'contributing to the delinquency of a minor.'"

"And what do they call infecting a man with invisible parasites?"

"Before you get on your high horse," Steven said, "that was done to benefit you."

"Yeah, well, watching Daniel die at the edge of the lake didn't seem like much of a benefit."

"You'll never get a free beer out of me that way," Steven said, returning to his menu.

The server showed up and they both placed an order.

"Sorry," Jason said after the server left. "I didn't mean to get off on the wrong foot. I'm just a little shaken by that whole thing. And the blow up between you and Grandpa Roy."

"That's all been patched up," Steven lied. "We mutually apologized and we've moved on."

"It's not like you and Grandpa Roy were ever close, anyway," Jason said.

"That's true. But things have changed in the past few months. We're closer now than we've ever been."

"Something changed?"

The server arrived with their drinks. Steven paused until the server had left.

"Yes," Steven said. "It changed. I had an incident at my house. Several months ago. Roy helped me resolve it."

"What kind of incident?"

"Well, how about we just call it an 'unusual incident' and leave it at that?"

"Dad," Jason said, "I don't think I really want to have this conversation if you're only going to be half-open with me. I'm not some little kid that needs protecting."

"If you'd seen the things I've seen in the past little while," Steven said, "you might disagree."

"Let me be the judge."

Steven took a long sip of his iced tea and leaned back into the cushions of the booth. He looked at Jason, who was staring back at him, almost a challenge. *Do I protect him?* he thought. *Is leaving him in the dark the best way to protect him? Or does that put him at greater risk?*

"When I moved into the house," Steven said, "I began seeing things at night. I'd be woken up in the middle of the night by knockings in the house. Then I'd see things, horrible things. I thought I was going crazy. I thought I had a brain tumor. Roy stepped in. He told me that I was fine, but the house was haunted. So we went about getting rid of the ghosts. It's a long story. But over the course of it I found out a lot of things about myself and your grandpa."

"Ghosts and haunted houses don't sound like you," Jason said, adding a couple of sugar packets to his iced tea. "You're the most rational person I know. Remember when I brought home that book on UFOs? I thought you were going to go bonkers."

"Trust me, I tried every rational explanation. Then I ran into some facts that changed my mind."

"Such as?"

"The River, for one."

"Ah, you mentioned that the other night."

"Have you ever gone in it?" Steven asked.

"Gone in it? I don't understand."

"Jumped into it. Let yourself drift mentally until you fall into it. That's what it feels like for me."

"No, I don't even know what you're talking about. Seriously, Dad, if you could hear yourself."

"I understand how it sounds. I'll stop if you're finding this too hard to believe."

"It's hard to believe, but continue, please."

"OK, so the River was one thing. Roy's abilities and his book were another."

"Grandpa Roy wrote a book?"

"It's a book he's added to, but it came from his father, and his father, and so on. Several generations."

"What's in it?"

"A history of all the weird shit they've dealt with over the years. You wouldn't believe it."

Now Jason looked interested, and a little stunned.

"Weird shit? Like what?"

"You name it. Ghosts, evil spirits, demons, creatures, the whole lot."

"Grandpa Roy wrote this?"

"Some of it, yes."

"And he's writing about his experiences?"

"Yes."

"And the purpose of the book, he's going to give it to you?"

"Yes, someday I expect."

"Then you'll start writing in it?"

"Yes, I guess I will."

"And does that mean that someday it comes to me?"

"I don't know. I suppose that's up to you, and to me."

The server arrived with their food, and passed out extra napkins and condiments. "Anything else I can get you?" she asked.

"Nope, looks good," Jason said.

"She's cute," Steven said as their server walked away.

Jason gave him a pathetic glance and went about eating his French fries.

"I see you still eat the French fries first," Steven said.

"The best part."

"So, anyway, after Roy helped me with my house problem, he and I went down to Oregon and helped some friends of his. They own a bed and breakfast outside of Medford, but it's far bigger than any B&B you've ever been to. Built in 1850. And full of ghosts. That's when I met Eliza."

"Oh," Jason said around bites of food. "I like her."

"Yes, everybody likes her."

"And Daniel? How did you meet him?"

"He's a friend…was a friend of Eliza's. When you and I were attacked in our sleep last week, I called Eliza for help because your grandpa was out boating with a friend of his. She referred me to Daniel. He was an expert in everything time related. It was Daniel who helped me figure out about Frank and how to eliminate him."

"And who exactly is Frank?" Jason asked.

Steven backtracked and filled Jason in on the recent events that had lead up to Daniel's death.

"So you saw something come out of Daniel's head, at the lake?" Jason asked.

"I entered the flow. I suspected something was happening that we couldn't see. Things had been so strange, his odd obsession with water since he was revived. As he was walking to the water, he kept saying he couldn't control himself. At first I thought it was Sean, but when he kneeled down and bent over, it felt like something else was happening, so I jumped into the River. The stalk coming out of his head was unlike anything I've ever seen."

"A stroma," Jason said. "It's called a stroma."

"What's that?"

"I learned it in Biology class. They come out of insects and animals after they've been used by parasites. They're called 'zombie parasites' because they control the body of the host, usually getting it to do something so they can reproduce. I've seen pictures of huge stalks coming out of ant's heads, really gross. And many of them drive their host to water, since they need water to reproduce."

"Christ, it appears I'm getting something for my money," Steven said. "This was all from a biology class?"

"In high school, Dad. I'm not taking any life sciences in college."

"Still, that's impressive. I've never heard of zombie parasites before."

"Here, hold on." Jason removed his phone and began typing in a browser. Soon he turned the phone to Steven, showing him the pictures. Steven saw the ant and an impossibly long stalk shooting out of its head.

"It was kind of like that," Steven said. "It came up out of him, bent at one point at about a ninety degree angle towards the water, and had a bulb on the end where the seeds came out."

"Yup, zombie parasite."

"I'm guessing the centipedes laid eggs in him?" Steven asked.

"I'm guessing that too," Jason said, taking the phone back. "These parasites have weird life cycles. And who knows since yours were invisible. *Invisible*. Do you know how freaky it feels to say that word with a straight face?"

"I felt the same way when I was first learning all this," Steven said. "I'm still a little shocked at some of the things I run into. I shouldn't be, but I am. I've been a skeptic my whole life, it's hard to get rid of."

"Well, I was never a skeptic," Jason said. "I wanted to read that UFO book. I ate it up."

"See, even now I discount the idea. Ghosts, yes. UFOs, no. I know, it makes no sense."

"So were you going to tell me about this?" Jason said, finishing his burger. Steven hadn't even started his yet.

"Eventually," Steven said. "I thought I'd wait until you were at least out of college and settled. Roy didn't introduce it to me until now, and look at me, I'm in my fifties. He wasn't in any rush so I figured I didn't need to be with you."

"How old was Grandpa Roy when his father told him?"

"Twelve, fourteen, something like that."

"Why do you think he waited so long to tell you?"

"We were never close. Your grandma made me and your Uncle Bernie go to church frequently. She saw it as a way to keep us safe from Roy's abilities. She helped create a gulf between me and Roy. One I regret."

"Maybe he felt you were too skeptical, too. Like you wouldn't believe it if he told you."

"Yes, that was probably part of it. Even when he did tell me I didn't believe it. It took a while. Seeing ghosts in my house sped the process along." Steven smiled.

"So what happens next?" Jason asked. "You going to train me?"

"You'd want that?"

"Sure, why not. Seems like it's a birthright or something. Wouldn't want to let the family down."

"I guess you could benefit from Roy. I'm still learning from him. No reason you couldn't jump in and learn too. But I worry about you. That's the main reason I didn't want to tell you about this. It's been dangerous, as you saw. Roy and I have come across some very dangerous and evil people and creatures."

"Ooo, sounds like a scary horror movie!"

Steven sighed. Jason was taking it cavalierly, which was exactly what he'd been afraid of. It would take an experience or two before he'd take it seriously. It was too late now; no putting the toothpaste back in the tube.

"Before we can do anything with Roy," Steven said. "We need him to come back safely. He's put his life on the line with this. If he fails, he won't come back."

"When will you know?" Jason said, sipping the last of his iced tea.

"I don't know how long it will take. Maybe a day or two. Maybe longer. We just have to wait and see."

"You'll let me know? When he's back?"

"I will," Steven said, lying. If Roy was successful, he knew it was a promise he'd never have to fulfill.

Fifteen

Roy had been concealed behind the junk pile in the garage for over an hour, waiting for the boys to enter the garage with Frank. As he waited, he attempted to communicate with Sam. It had been difficult.

Sam was distrustful of anyone Roy's age. Roy tried to explain the wooden matchbox and powder would work but only for a while, and that many others would be hurt later on when Frank broke free of the cage. He told Sam that he'd convinced David to play it another way instead of using the items, and that they'd be in the garage soon. He told Sam that David intended to kill Frank when they got to the garage, to protect Sean and Garth.

Sam had not been very communicative. Roy didn't know if he approved of the plan or if he was ignoring him all along since he didn't acknowledge much of what Roy was saying. Roy had begged him to help David if he could, once they arrived in the garage. Sam didn't say he would.

After a while the conversation stopped. Roy told Sam he'd wait for the boys to arrive by hiding behind the pile. Sam didn't say anything in return.

The garage was silent. The musty smell of cut grass mixed with the smell of burnt wood and creosote. It was a smell Roy remembered from similar buildings in his youth. He always associated that smell with spiders.

David appeared in the doorway of the garage. He looked around, waiting for his eyes to adjust.

"Davy," Roy called. "Back here."

David walked inside the garage and tentatively towards Roy's voice. Once he made his way around the junk pile, he saw Roy crouched down near the floor. He also sensed the presence that was with Roy, listening.

Roy saw David's reaction, his fear. David was more susceptible to the flow than he realized. The demon was scaring him off.

"I… I don't know if I should do this, mister," David said, backing away a little.

"You're scaring the boy, it'll ruin the plan!" Roy told the demon.

"I've been waiting a long time, much longer than usual," the demon said, his voice rumbling in the lowest registers they could hear. "I want my payment."

"Your payment comes after Davy shoots Frank," Roy said. "Not before. We talked about this."

"It looks like your father is having a change of heart," the demon said. "If he fails, I'll take you so quickly you won't realize it happened."

"What is he?" David asked, taking another step back. "He's not human."

"No," Roy said. "He isn't. He brought me here so I could help you solve this."

"He called me your father," David said. "Those weren't visions, were they?"

"You're right, they weren't visions. That's what actually happens in the future."

"And I am your father?"

"Yes," Roy said, "you are. You are my father. You named me Roy."

David looked like he wanted to bolt from the room, but he didn't move.

"If I don't do this, what happens, in the future?"

"Frank comes back after several years, attacking me, my son, and his son."

"I'm a grandfather, and a great-grandfather?"

"Yes, and they're all grateful to you for what you did, what you pass on from your father, all of it. But we won't be around if you don't do this."

"And him?" David asked, pointing at the demon.

"He was the only way I could come back here and talk to you. He will take Frank's soul as payment for bringing me here, if you kill him. If you don't, he'll take me instead."

Roy felt he'd put every compelling reason on the table that he could. It was a mixture of truth and lies, all designed to get David to pull the trigger. Any more and he'd be pushing too hard, increasing the risk that David might back out. He stopped and looked at David with as desperate an expression as he could muster.

"Is that true?" David asked the demon.

"It is," the demon answered. "I will be paid, one way or the other. And I won't wait much longer."

David looked at Roy. From inside the house they could hear screaming, a mixture of the boys yelping and Frank's loud, booming voice. They could hear things smashing. Then they heard the sound of the kitchen door opening and slamming shut, and the rapid fall of approaching footsteps.

"They're here," Roy said. "Now it's your choice, Davy. Frank, or me."

David removed the pistol from his back belt where he'd concealed it under his shirt.

"Do you know how to use it?" Roy asked.

"I think so," he said.

"Come hide here with me in the shadows. Once Frank comes in you can use it on him. He'll be blind for the first few moments when he walks in as his eyes adjust to the darkness. That's the time."

David joined Roy behind the junk pile, pistol in hand. It was large in his hand, and heavy. Roy saw the gun droop a bit as he held it.

"Use both hands," he whispered to David as Garth came running into the garage. He was crying and breathing hard.

"Davy, you here?" Garth said, trying to catch his breath.

"Yeah, I'm here," David said.

"Good. Sean is on his way. Frank is madder than a hornet's nest."

Within a moment Sean came running into the garage. He had a black eye and blood was running from a cut on his cheek.

"Did he see you come out here?" Garth asked.

"Yes, he saw me," Sean said. "Is Davy here?"

"Yes, he's here," Garth said. "What do we do?"

"I don't know," Sean said. "Davy, what do we do?"

"Hide," said David, emerging from the back of the junk pile, holding the pistol.

Sean and Garth saw the gun and their eyes went wide. They both scrambled for hiding places.

"You come back here, you little shitheads!" Frank bellowed from the house. "If I have to come out there and get you, you'll be sorry!"

Roy could hear Garth whimper. Sean and Garth were out of his line of sight, but he could see David, who had moved into position near the door. He held the gun at arm's length, ready to fire as soon as Frank entered the building.

"I'm gonna count to three," Frank yelled. "You know what happens at three!"

Roy wondered what exactly Frank had done to the boys in the past. From Garth's story that Steven had relayed to him, it sounded pretty horrible. He didn't regret what was about to happen.

"One!" Frank hollered.

The garage was silent.

"Two!"

Roy heard Garth whimper again. It made him regret ever having spanked Steven or Bernie as they grew up.

What an asshole I am for not reconciling with Steven before coming here, Roy thought. *I may never see him again. What a monumental prick I can be sometimes.*

"Three! Ready or not, here I come!"

He could see a gulp go down David's throat as he steeled himself for the confrontation. He could hear the demon next to him, panting, readying himself for the soul that was coming his way within moments. Sean and Garth were nowhere to be seen, tucked into spaces only they knew.

Frank's long shadow reached the doorway before he did.

"You two shitheads need to learn some respect," he said, just outside the doorway. "I'm gonna burn it into ya." They could hear Frank flicking his lighter. "Just imagine, Garth – Sean with his hair on fire. All his hair burned off his head.

Wouldn't that look funny? I'll bet you'll shit your pants laughing at him."

He flicked the lighter more.

"There's no way out of this, boys. Come on out now. You come out now, I'll only beat you until you're black and blue. You make me come in there, I'm gonna beat you so hard you won't know who you are. And then I'll burn ya."

He flicked the lighter a few more times. Roy was afraid the boys would cave and go out to him, but they didn't. The garage was silent except for the sound of Frank's lighter clicking away the seconds. Then it stopped.

"Fine, have it your way." He walked into the garage.

David raised the pistol, pointing it at Frank's chest. *Now,* Roy thought. *Pull the trigger now!*

David pulled the trigger, but no shot came out. The gun only clicked.

Frank heard the click and turned to look in the direction of the sound. He saw the barrel of the gun and the face behind it.

"You!" he said, marching towards David at full speed.

David was stunned that the gun hadn't worked. He pulled the trigger again. This time Frank had reached him and had his hand below the barrel. As David pulled, Frank raised his hand, bringing the barrel of the gun upwards. The bullet left the gun and grazed Frank's scalp. Blood began to run down his face.

Frank paused for a moment, but once he realized he wasn't dead, he went into a frenzy. He easily wrestled the gun from David's hands as David tried to pull off another shot. Once he had the gun, he ran at David, pinning him against the wall of the garage. With his left hand he held David's chest against the wall, and with his right he held the gun. Then he brought the handle of the gun down against David's face, pistol-whipping him. Frank's face was dripping blood from the wound on his head, and the blood was running down onto his chest. He raised the gun again and brought it down on David. David let out a scream, which faltered and sputtered as blood from his own wounds gagged his throat.

David raised his feet and kicked at Frank as hard as he could. It was enough to knock Frank back a few inches, which was just enough to relieve the pressure on David from Frank's left hand, and David slid down the wall of the garage to the floor. Frank took a step back to catch his breath and wipe the blood from his eyes. David took the opportunity to try and crawl away, but Frank brought his foot down on David's hand. Roy could hear the bones of David's hand break.

Do something! Roy thought. But he couldn't do anything, couldn't touch anything or make anything happen. He was helpless.

Garth flew out from his hiding place, pounding on Frank from behind. He had little effect. Frank turned and grabbed Garth by the shirt and threw him against the garage wall. Garth hit the wall and fell to the floor, stunned. David continued to crawl away, favoring his unbroken hand. Frank kicked him in the stomach, raising his body off the ground by two feet. David fell to the floor in a heap, the wind literally kicked out of him, unable to move.

Frank moved back into position over David, raising his foot over David's back.

He'll break his back, Roy thought. *Please, god, someone do something!*

Suddenly the room was brightly lit, as though hundreds of lights had turned on all at once. Everyone in the room was still, frozen in place. Except for Sean.

Roy saw the extended hand from the junk pile with Sean next to it. Sean stood, the only one able to move. He walked over to the wall of the garage where tools and implements were hanging. He removed a pitchfork and walked over to Frank. Frank was frozen in place. Sean positioned the tines of the pitchfork at Frank's back. Suddenly the brightness of the room vanished and the garage was returned to its normal light. Frank continued to raise his leg, ready to bring it down on David's back.

Sean pushed the pitchfork into Frank. He pushed until the tines emerged from the other side. Then he pulled the pitchfork out and shoved it in again. Roy felt the demon next to him begin to materialize.

Frank turned. Sean let go of the pitchfork. As Frank turned, the pitchfork swung around behind him. Frank snarled down at Sean, his face so completely covered with blood that it was impossible to see his features. He lunged at Sean, sliding off the tines of the pitchfork; behind Frank, Garth had grabbed hold of the pitchfork's handle. Frank fell on top of Sean, the blood of his wound dripping down onto Sean's head and face. Frank leaned back and brought his arm up to swing at Sean. Sean turned his head away from the impending blow and waited for it to hit. But it never came.

He turned back to look at Frank on top of him. Garth had run the pitchfork through his neck from behind. Frank was trying to breathe but was only sputtering instead, bubbles of blood forming on his mouth as he tried to exhale. He fell off Sean to the side, his hands reaching for the tines of the pitchfork, but unable to remove them. Sean got to his feet and went to Garth, who was still holding the handle of the pitchfork. Garth shoved the handle at Frank again for good measure. They heard Frank gasping and knew he was done for. They both went to David to see if he was OK.

Roy felt the demon leave his side and swiftly move over to Frank. Roy entered the flow. He saw the demon lower its large head next to Frank's, eyeing the final moments of Frank's life as he struggled to breathe and the blood poured out of his wounds. The demon looked like an animal waiting for the opportune moment to strike its prey. That moment came within seconds, and the demon opened its mouth. Roy saw the exact second when Frank heaved his last sigh and the demon sucked his soul away.

Roy exited the flow and walked out from behind the junk pile and over to David. The boys seemed too shocked to question why he was there. He checked on David and saw that he was breathing. Aside from some nasty cuts to his face and his broken hand, he was OK.

"Boys," Roy said, "run across the street and tell Davy's mother what happened. You boys killed Frank in self-defense, remember that. Sean and David's wounds should prove that. And make sure he gets his pocket knife back from under Frank's bed."

Sean and Garth backed away from David and Roy, then ran out of the garage.

"Are we done here?" the demon asked, still standing next to Frank's dead body.

"One more thing," Roy said, and walked over to the junk pile. "Thank you, Sam. I owe you one."

Sixteen

Roy found himself back in an empty house. No Steven, no Eliza waiting for him to return. At first he was pissed they weren't there, upset they'd leave him while he was occupied with such an important task. Then he realized they hadn't left him; they'd simply never been there to begin with.

He went to the phone and called Steven.

"Hello, how are you feeling?" Roy asked.

"Fine, and you?"

"Fine, fine. Any trouble sleeping last night?"

"No, no trouble there. The ghosts have been gone for months, Dad."

"Heard from Jason lately?"

"As a matter of fact, I have," Steven said. "He and I are getting together for a dinner this weekend. Why don't you join us?"

"Sure, no problem, sounds like fun. So...everything's fine?"

"As far as I know. Why? Is something wrong?"

"No, nothing," Roy said. "Sounds like everything's good. Talk to you later."

"Goodbye, Dad."

Roy hung up the phone. Next he tried Eliza.

"Hello, Eliza? It's Roy."

"Well, Roy!" she said. "How good to hear your voice, it's been so long. How have you been? All busy practicing being handsome, I expect."

Eliza, Roy thought. *So easy to like.*

"Well, I guess it has been a while," he said. "How long has it been, exactly, since we saw each other last?"

"Three months?" Eliza said. "Something like that, at Pete and Sarah's. When are you gonna come down for a visit and bring that son of yours?"

"Soon, Eliza, soon," Roy said. "Hey, I need a favor. I'm wondering if you would point me in the right direction with something."

"Sure, what is it?"

"Well, I'm in need of some advice from someone who knows a lot about time, time-related things, that type of stuff."

"I've got just the person," Eliza said. "His name is Daniel and he lives in Spokane. He's a friend of mine. Knows more about time than anyone I know."

"Perfect," Roy said, "would you mind referring me to him? I'd like to talk to him about something I've discovered, see if he has any insight on it."

"Sure, why don't I give him a call right now, and then you call him in half an hour?"

"Sounds good, what's his number?"

Roy jotted down the number Eliza gave him, thanked her and assured her he'd plan a visit soon, and hung up. Then he waited forty-five minutes for good measure and called Daniel to invite him over to Seattle. He had somewhere he wanted to take him.

◊

"I can't say I'm comfortable with this," Daniel said as Roy led him down the dark hallway of the church. "It's bad enough breaking and entering, but a church? This seems wrong."

"Trust me," Roy said, "you'll think you've hit the lottery when I show you what's down here."

Roy led him to the door with the padlock. Roy removed a pair of bolt cutters from his bag and clipped the padlock off.

"I hope you're right," Daniel said. "We could get into a lot of trouble for this."

"No, not really," Roy said. "We're not going to take anything, and even if we get caught, I know the owner."

They twisted their way through the basement of the church, Roy shining his flashlight ahead of them. They stopped at a pile of boxes near the back of the basement. Roy pointed his flashlight at the corner of the room, casting enough ambient light to illuminate the boxes.

"This is what you wanted to show me? What we broke in here for?" Daniel asked.

"Wait," Roy said. "Just wait. Sam?"

Roy stared at the gaps between the boxes where light didn't penetrate. "Sam? Are you in there? It's me, Roy. Do you remember me?"

A pale face appeared in one of the gaps. Daniel gasped when he saw it. He gasped again when he saw the face change age, from a young man to a toddler.

"Yes," the boy said. "I remember. The garage. Sean and Garth."

"I brought you something," Roy said. "Do you remember these?"

Roy opened his hand, holding the wooden matchbox and the envelope of powder.

"Yes," the boy said. "I remember. I gave those to Davy."

"I thought you should have them back," Roy said, "since Davy never used them. They were yours. And I wanted to thank you for what you did back then. You saved my father's life."

"Davy was your father," the boy said, changing from a toddler to a six year old. "I remember. He let you get old."

"Sam, there's someone I'd like you to meet," Roy said, backing up and extending his arm to Daniel. "His name is Daniel. He knows a lot about time."

"Hello, Daniel," the boy said. "Pleased to meet you."

"Hello, Sam," Daniel said.

"Sam wants to be younger," Roy said. "It's all he wants, more than anything else. He's found a way to become younger for a few seconds at a time, but it doesn't last."

"Why do you want to be younger?" Daniel asked Sam.

"So my mother will love me," the boy said. "She wants a baby, not a boy. Can you help me?"

"You've found a way to become younger already, I see," Daniel said.

"Yes," Sam said. "Martha's friends helped me. Look."

Sam rapidly changed from a small infant to a ten year old, morphing through all ages in between.

"But I can't stay anything but ten for very long."

"You just need a stabilizer," Daniel said. "If you use the stabilizer when you're the age you want to be, it'll stick."

"How do I get a stabilizer?" the boy asked.

"I have several at home," Daniel said. "I'll give you one."

"Oh, would you? That would be so kind of you, I would be so grateful."

"Sure, I'll bring it to you the next time I visit here."

"How soon will that be?"

"Well, I do live a ways away. It takes me a day to drive home and another to drive back."

"Would it help if I gave you these?" the boy said, and the pale arm extended from the pile, holding two objects. Daniel took them from the open palm and the arm retreated back inside the pile.

"Wow," Daniel said. "These are magnificent! But you don't have to give me these, I'll bring you the stabilizer regardless."

"If you do, I'll become a baby again, and my mother will take me away. I want you to have all of my collection. Martha's friends gave me lots of things like those. You can have them all, because if I'm a baby, I won't need them anymore."

Daniel turned to look at Roy.

"Told you," Roy said.

"I'll bring you back the stabilizer," Daniel said. "Right away. And thank you, Sam."

"Oh, thank you, you don't know how happy I am now. Please hurry back as soon as you can."

The boy's face faded, and Roy grabbed Daniel by the shoulder.

"Show me what he gave you," Roy said. Daniel held the items up for Roy to see.

"Good. When you get access to the rest of his stuff, do not – and I mean *do not* – open a carved box about yea big," he held his hand up to illustrate the size. "And keep an eye on the rest of that stuff. That box is dangerous, and the other items might be too."

"I'll be careful," Daniel said. "But you can't imagine what a find this is. I collect rare time objects, you know."

"Yes, I know," Roy said.

"This looks like it might be a chronosphere. I've never seen one before, in person."

"Come on, let's get out of here."

◊

Roy drove Daniel back to his car so he could return to Spokane with his prizes. The drive from Marysville to Seattle would take an hour, and Roy realized it would be filled with Daniel's enthusiastic thanks and observations about Sam and the items he might possess. Daniel knew a long list of rare time-related items, many of which he'd only read or heard about, and he imagined them all potentially being in Sam's pile. He was like a kid who'd just been taken to Disneyland, and he wanted to go back.

Roy listened to Daniel for a while, then began to tune out, nodding enough to keep Daniel thinking he was listening, but not really paying attention to what he was saying. He'd just returned from a timeline that was now gone, with Frank's return and Daniel's death obliterated. None of those things happened in the timeline he was now participating in, and he was a little unsure if everything he remembered from birth onward had actually happened in this new timeline. It appeared they had, but there should be tiny differences. Everyone still answered the same phone numbers, buildings were still in the same places, and relationships seemed the same. Steven still had a son named Jason.

Now that Jason's unfortunate exposure to the River was also gone, Roy felt Steven had a new chance to present things to Jason correctly, so he could understand the power and responsibility having "the gift" entailed. He'd waited way too long to present it to Steven, and he felt Steven needed to speak to Jason about it soon, to give him a chance to learn about it at a younger age.

Steven had been right. Leaving things unresolved may have seemed like a good idea at the time, but his encounter with Frank reminded him that sometimes evil had to be stamped out completely, not left to return. If there was any hope of getting Steven to talk to Jason sooner rather than later, Roy would need to find a way to resolve these problems from the past.

Problems from the past, Roy thought. You don't often get a chance to go back and correct problems from the past. You usually have to live with the consequences of the present moment, which could be cruel and unforgiving. *I was lucky. I got to correct this one,* he thought. *I need to correct others as soon as I can.* He felt like a man who'd lived through a near-death experience and was being given a second chance to live his life differently.

Daniel was still talking, and Roy would normally be annoyed, but he wasn't. He was happy to hear Daniel's voice, pleased that the plan worked. The alternative would have been much worse for everyone, including himself. Daniel talking his ear off in his car meant they won, they pulled it off. And Roy now had an opportunity to set some things right.

My time will come soon, Roy thought. It was always out there, the frustrating thoughts about what would happen when his time was up and he was forced to move on. He tried not to think about them, tried not to be scared by them, but the thoughts came with more regularity these days than they did in the past, now that Steven was aware of his gift and was using it. *I need to accelerate things,* he thought. *Can't waste time.*

Daniel was going on about something "on a molecular level." Roy smiled and nodded, continuing to feign interest. *Why not start now?* he thought. *The present moment is all I've got. Why not live it to the fullest?*

He stopped thinking about the future and returned to the discussion of time objects, time dilation, and spatial symmetry. Daniel was brilliant, and Roy was determined to learn something from him, to make this hour-long car ride count.

After all, wasn't that the point? To make the present moment count?

He leaned back in the seat and listened.

Michael Richan lives in Seattle, Washington.

◊

Visit

www.michaelrichan.com

for more information about the books in The River series.

◊

Did you enjoy this book?

The author would love to know your opinion of the book.

Please leave your review at Amazon.com, Goodreads.com, or your online retailer. Your feedback is appreciated!

23508556R00139

Made in the USA
Charleston, SC
25 October 2013